D1027278

RUSTLER'S TRAIL

Jim Carlin knew he would have to stand up and fight before he could settle down in Beaver Tail, because he had staked his claim right in the middle of Big Ike Outland's best grass. But Outland wasn't the only score he had to settle. Jim's renegade brother was also in Beaver Tail, and that meant Jim had to pay off an old debt with his new gun—or never live to fire it . . .

LEE FLOREN

RUSTLER'S TRAIL

Complete and Unabridged

LINFORD
Leicester

First published in the USA in 1964 by
Paperback Library Books,
USA

First Linford Edition
published January 1988

British Library CIP Data

Floren, Lee
Rustler's trail.—Large print ed.—
Linford western library
I. Title
813'.52[F] PS3511.L697

ISBN 0-7089-6485-0

Published by
F. A. Thorpe (Publishing) Ltd.
Anstey, Leicestershire
Set by Rowland Phototypesetting Ltd.
Bury St. Edmunds, Suffolk
Printed and bound in Great Britain by
T. J. Press (Padstow) Ltd., Padstow, Cornwall

1

THE county-clerk peered at the big wall-map. Finally he laid an inky index-finger against it. "This the place where you aim to take up a homestead, Stranger?"

Jim Carlin said, "Can't see good from here," and came around the corner of the counter.

"Nobody but people on official business are allowed behind the counter, sir."

Jim smiled. "My business is official." He walked over to the map. "You're pointin' at Dog Crick, fella. The piece of land I aim to file on is over here on Hell Crick." The lanky cowboy studied the map carefully and let his thumb land on a spot. "This's it; right here."

"Dog Crick has better land."

Jim said, "I aim to file on Hell Crick." He smiled again and ran a rope-calloused hand through brick red hair. He was six-two, just about half a foot higher than the clerk. But what the clerk lacked in height he made up in girth. Jim's belly and flanks were as flat as a board.

"I still say there is better farmin' land on Dog Crick."

Jim's smile became suddenly severe. "Mister, who's takin' up this homestead —me or you?"

"Get yourself killed off if you wanta, Stranger. Me, I'm jes' tryin' to save your neck for you. Big Ike Outland finds out you're takin' up a homestead smack dab in his range an' he'll land on you. Big Ike drove cattle into this section right after the last fracas an' he ain't gonna let no nester sit on his range—"

"Well said, clerk!" The voice was harsh and it came from the open doorway.

The clerk turned and stared at the big man who had entered so silently. His jaw hung open and he said, "Shucks, Big Ike himself!" He looked suddenly at Jim Carlin, who had also turned.

Carlin saw a man almost his own

height. But where Jim Carlin had the wiry suppleness of his early twenties this man had the corpulent strength of his late thirties. Already a gray tinge touched the iron-sorrel hair that showed from under the rim of his big Stetson. The only thing they had in common was their height. For Jim Carlin's face was still youthful, almost boyish; the face of Big Ike Outland was marked by predatory emotions, grooved by the man's nature. The years had not left their mark on Jim Carlin's strong face as they had on the sneering countenance of the big man. One glance was all that it took to spot Ike Outland as an unscrupulous land-grabber, a man who was out for all he could get. And this man wanted plenty. No fast-riding youth from Texas was going to do him out of all the land that he had taken years to acquire. The fact that it had all been acquired at the cost of many men's lives mattered little to Big Ike. What was important was that he owned the property and while he was alive and kicking, he intended to hang on to it!

Big Ike Outland looked at Jim. "Fellow was in here loafin' when you come in, Stranger. He done heard you talkin' with this clerk an' he scooted down to the saloon to tell me you aimed to take up a homestead on my graze."

"You must have quite a spy system, Outland."

Big Ike Outland had no answer to that. He came around the corner of the counter and the clerk did not remind him that only those with official business were allowed behind the desk.

"Where's this land at this hellion aims to squat on, clerk?"

"Right here." The clerk's finger found Hell Creek.

Jim's smile had changed into a tough grin. "Clerk," he said, shaking his head in feigned disgust, "can't you remember nothin' at all? I don't aim to file on Hell Crick at that particular point. My homestead is over here to the west. That would be the Big Horn Meridian, Range 35 North, Township 14, Section 17, the way I read this map."

"You mean—" Big Ike Outland's thumb left a greasy spot on the map. "—you aim to settle right there?"

"That's the spot."

Big Ike Outland's green-gray eyes peered at Jim as though their owner was scrutinizing a strange object he had never seen before.

"Stranger, are you in your right mind?"

"I figure so. Why ask?"

"That spot where you aim to homestead is my best grass."

"You ain't got no deeds to that strip," Jim pointed out. "You're jes' like the rest of the cowmen—you moved in cattle and claim land you have no legal right to claim."

"Maybe I ain't got a legal right but I got a six-shooter right!"

"Legal right wins in a court of law."

"Look, fella, you look sensible enough. They's plenty of good homestead land north of here. Why not move on?"

"I settle there."

Big Ike Outland growled, "You won't move, eh?"

"Nope, sir. I'm filin' first papers."

Boots sounded and both looked at the open door. A squat, ugly toad of a man, almost as wide as he was tall, stood in the doorway. He chewed tobacco rhythmically and he toted two guns, both tied down to his beefy hams.

"You havin' troubles, boss?"

"Toad, this gent aims to take up a homestead on Hell Crick. I'm tryin' to get him to move on."

Toad Graham's heavily-lidded eyes, opened to mere slits, swiveled around and settled on Jim Carlin.

"He looks like a sensible critter to me, Big Ike. He'll have sense enough to keep on movin' north, I figure."

"He claims he won't move," Big Ike Outland growled.

"Then move him," Toad grunted.

And Big Ike Outland, without a bit of warning, swung on Jim Carlin!

Carlin tried to duck, but he was too late. The unexpectedness of the cowardly attack was too fast. Big Ike Outland's knuckles hit him on the left cheek. Jim almost fell over the clerk, who was scurrying out of range. As it was, the clerk held him up; otherwise, the blow would have dropped him.

Carlin's head rang, and his sight was misty. But he saw Big Ike coming in on him and he ducked the second blow—a round-house right. Anger came in and swept the cobwebs of surprise to one side. The next time Big Ike swung, Jim Carlin landed a hard fist in the man's belly. It must have done some damage, for he heard Big Ike grunt. And he thought it slowed the cowman down a little.

He was certain of one thing: he was in a fight for his life. He circled, bumped into a swivel chair; he kicked it and it rolled over. Somewhere the clerk was hollering something about "wrecking the furniture!" Carlin grinned through bloody lips. He grunted, "Come on, cowman, come on!"

He thought he detected a surprised look on Big Ike Outland's beefy face.

Evidently Big Ike had used his fists before without warning. But previously, evidently, his victim had dropped immediately. Now he seemed worried and surprised because he, Jim Carlin, was still on his boots.

"Get him, Big Ike!"

That was Toad's voice, encouraging his boss.

"Get Sheriff Albers!" The clerk's voice.

"Sit down, clerk!"

Jim glimpsed the clerk flying back toward the wall, his arms swinging vainly as he tried to grab a hand-hold on the thin air. Toad packed a hard left.

"Rest there, clerk!"

Big Ike smashed Jim across the mouth with a mauling right fist that stunned more than it hurt. Suddenly Jim feared he might not be able to take the big cowman. Sure, he was maybe ten years younger than Big Ike, but he had spotted the cowman about twenty pounds. And that big difference in weight was beginning to show.

He glimpsed an opening and he knocked Big Ike down.

When the cowman bounced up, he had a chair by the hind legs. He swung it. Jim Carlin ducked. The window broke with a loud noise.

Again the clerk hollered and again Toad knocked him down.

Jim backed into the desk. The edge of it was sharp across his spine. His right hand went back and grabbed a heavy paper weight. Big Ike came in—and Big Ike wasn't a pretty picture.

Jim could hear the rattle of the big man's breath. Big Ike's shirt was ripped and shreds of it hung from his collar. The rest of the shirt dangled in strings from his gun belt. He looked like an ape. His chest, black with wiry hair, was heavy and strong.

"Now I've got you, stranger!"

Using the desk for a brace, Jim whammed both boots into Big Ike's belly. But Big Ike, instead of going backwards, hung onto Jim's boots. His weight jerked Jim off the desk. They hit the floor and

Jim knew that if Big Ike ever got him down, if he ever got his full weight on him—well, the curtain would come down.

So he swung the paper weight.

It came down with a sickening crunch on Big Ike's sorrel-topped head. And the cowman folded up like a wind-broken accordion.

Jim rolled to one side. Big Ike hit the floor with a thud.

The clerk screamed, "He's kilt Big Ike."

Blood colored the sorrel hair and gave it a reddish tint.

Jim got to his feet, his knees weak. He had taken quite a bit of punishment himself. His knuckles ached.

Toad said, "Mister, you might think you've won this hand, but you ain't, not by a damn sight! Mister, I'm lettin' you look into my gun as the hammer falls!"

Jim saw the man's .45 level.

The clerk hollered, "Don't kill him in cold blood, Toad! Anyway, don't kill him in my office!"

"Close your tater trap, clerk."

Jim gasped for air. The .45 did not waver. He knew, from the narrowed set to Toad's eyes, that the man intended to kill him. Jim's right hand went to his holster. The holster was empty.

He had lost his Colt in the fight!

Toad said, "This is it, Stranger!" and Jim heard the .45's hammer click back.

A thousand plans, all wild and disjointed, ran through Jim Carlin's brain. He realized he still held the paper weight. Desperately, he flung it at Toad. The man moved a pace to one side. The paper weight broke a window and went out into the street.

Toad grinned.

"Funny boy, eh?"

Jim thought, "This is it!" And the irony of it all struck him with full significance. Here he had come into Beaver Tail to file on a homestead and he'd never ride out of this town alive!

Suddenly a pair of big hands came from behind Toad to anchor themselves firmly around his thick neck. They must have had the strength of a work horse for the man struggled to get loose. Behind those big hands was a man with shoulders even wider than those of Toad.

"Tough boy eh?"

Toad let the hammer of the .45 drop. The lead tore into the floor harmlessly. He threshed and twisted, trying to turn. He couldn't make it.

Jim Carlin gasped, "You came jus' in time, Bootjack."

"Anythin' to accommodate you, Jim."

Jim tried to smile. The world went on a sudden pivot, swinging around and around, and it sucked him into its mad vortex. The last he remembered was that the floor joined the maelstrom, too—and it hit him smack in the face!

2

"OUCH!"

A Gros Ventres Indian buck was in Jim's head and the buck was pounding on his tom-tom. Jim realized his shirt was all wet; in fact, he seemed wet all over. Despite his aching head his eyes cleared.

He was sitting on Beaver Tail's main-street in front of the watering-trough. Behind him the windmill lifted water with a shrill sound.

"That windmill needs oil."

"What you say, Jim?"

His eyes cleared enough to see that Bootjack James stood over him. Concern and worry were written on the big man's wide face. Jim also noted that Bootjack held a pail full of water.

"Hey, no more water! I'm wet to the skin now!"

"I won't throw any more."

"How do you feel, sir?"

The words came from Jim's right. He swiveled his head around and almost blinked his eyes in amazement. She had one of those soft, comfortable voices, and she looked even lovelier than her voice. She wasn't more than five feet tall and she had blonde hair that rebelliously peeped from under her cream-colored Stetson. A silk blouse and a buckskin vest failed to hide her feminine charms. Jim liked her blue eyes. He wasn't much of a hand for thinking up nice words but he finally decided her eyes were china blue.

"Maybe I am dead," he said.

She said, "Shucks, I'm no angel. Sometimes I even swear." His head ached but still her laugh sounded good. "I'm Janet Albers."

Jim thought, "Albers, I've heard that name before," and he remembered that the clerk had hollered for Sheriff Albers.

"You the sheriff's wife, ma'am?"

"His daughter!"

Jim got to his feet. He felt better

standing up. "Shucks, I'm mightily all-fired glad to hear that, Janet."

"What a compliment!"

They all laughed and Jim remembered the fight in the clerk's office. His right hand sneaked up and explored his wet scalp. He had a big bump on his cranium. He had never seen an ostrich egg but he figured the bump was about the size of one. If not bigger . . .

"Who beaned me?"

Bootjack said, "The clerk come up behin' you, boss."

"That dirty little terrier! I'll twist him around until he can lick the bottom of his dirty feet!"

"No more fighting!" Janet Albers' voice was suddenly very stern.

Jim's scrutiny showed amusement. "Who says so?"

"I do, big gent! My father is out of town and while he's gone I'm the law here in Beaver Tail and I act on the orders of the county commissioners, savvy?"

Jim's smile died. "All right, honey."

"And don't *honey* me!"

"That's the first time you've ever called a sheriff *honey*," Bootjack opined. "Jim, you sure wrecked that office."

A pain ran through Jim's head and he openly winced. "Danged near wrecked me, too. How about that Toad fellow, Bootjack?"

Bootjack explained. He had brought up a big knee and planted it solidly in the area of Toad's left kidney. That had doubled the man. Then a solid right to the jaw had lifted Toad and dumped him in an unconscious pile of humanity.

"Well, you'd already knocked this Big Ike gent to sleep, so I totes you over here to this tank—"

"Yeah, an' you dumped it on me!"

"An' then this lawman—I mean law-woman—shows up."

"She's nice to look at," Jim allowed. "Where are those two big bad boys now, Bootjack?"

"They're in the doc's office. Doc said he wouldn't look at you 'cause you're a nester. They don't seem to cotton to us nesters, Jim."

Strength had returned to Jim's knees, but his head still held the Gros Ventre buck Indian and his tom-tom. He needed something that would kill that buck and he headed for the Singlebit Saloon.

"Wait a minute," Janet ordered.

"What'd you want to talk to me about?"

"Yourself, mister, yourself."

"Come into the saloon an' we'll gab."

"A woman can't go into the saloon!"

"Then we'll talk some other time."

She grabbed hold of his arm but he just moved ahead. "'T 'aint every man that has such a good lookin' woman draggin' onto him right after he hits a strange town," Jim told Bootjack. "Wonder what the rest of the burg thinks of this female? Tryin' to get a man so hard she hangs onto his arm!"

Janet dropped his arm like it was a red hot poker.

"I want to talk to you!"

Jim said, "Later, honey, later," and he and his partner entered the Singlebit. He went to the long bar and put down a buck. “Two shots of something strong, Aprons.”

But the beefy bartender shook his head. “Cain’t sell hard stuff to either Injuns or homesteaders, fella. Sorry.”

Jim studied him. “You mean that?”

“I’m not jokin!”

There were about four or five other men in the saloon and they played cards across the room. Jim glanced at them but they seemed vitally interested in their pasteboards.

“The gover’ment won’t let Injuns drink,” Jim Carlin said. “But who passed the law against a homesteader buyin’ a shot?”

“Big Ike Outland.”

“Outland own this bar?”

“No I own it. But Big Ike built this range into what it is an’ his word is good enough for me.”

“Well, well,” Jim said, “well, well.” He glanced at Bootjack.

“I sorta hate to do it,” Bootjack said. “He’s a stranger to me an’ I don’t hol’ much against him.”

The bartender had his right hand hidden under the bar. Jim knew that the fellow had grabbed hold of either a bung-starter or a billy-club.

Jim said, "Well, we gotta have a drink, pard."

Bootjack sighed. "All right, pal, here goes."

Both big hands went out and grabbed the bartender around the neck. Bodily the bartender was lifted off the floor, and he was not a small man. His right hand came up with a billy. He swung it and Jim caught it as it went overhead. One snap and he had it in his hand.

"Good work, Bootjack."

The bartender was swearing but his curses were muffled due to the pressure of Bootjack's hands. Bootjack pulled him across the bar, set him on his feet, and then gave his thick neck a sudden twist. The bartender went across the room. He hit the table where the men were playing cards. Chips, cards, table and players went flying.

"What the hell—?" One player gasped.

Bootjack looked at the man who sat in the sawdust. "Sorry I disturbed your game. I'm missing my aim, Jim. I aimed to send him out that window."

"Missed it by a foot," Jim growled.

Jim Carlin vaulted the bar, got a bottle from the shelf, and poured two jiggers of whiskey. The bartender had got to his feet and when Bootjack turned to down his drink he rushed him. But Bootjack saw him coming in the back bar mirror. He twisted and his whiskey went into the man's face. That stopped him. He stood and sputtered and cursed.

"I'll get a warrant for your arrest!" he threatened.

"Sit down," Bootjack ordered.

"I'll get—"

"Sit down or I'll—" Bootjack advanced, hands opening and closing. The bartender ran to a chair and sat down. Somebody laughed.

Jim Carlin said, "Belly up to the mahogany, men, an' drink on Jim Carlin, the first nester on Beaver Tail grass!"

"You're stealin' my whiskey!" the

bartender snapped. But he didn't get off the chair, Jim noticed.

Jim assured that he would pay for every drink. He had a solemn face as he told the bartender he was only tending bar because the bartender was unable to attend to his chores due to ill health. The bartender snarled back that he was well enough to pour whiskey.

"But your neck sir! You seem to be rubbin' it!"

"My neck is all right." The bartender cocked his head. "Ouch!" His glance at Bootjack James was not a sociable glance. "You wanta be careful, man; you could break a human's neck with them great big paws!"

"Maybe I have."

They all drank. Jim realized he was setting up drinks for a bunch of Beaver Tail's loafers. Despite his joking and his unconcerned face, the tall cowpuncher was slightly worried. Things had gone wrong from the moment he and Bootjack had ridden into this Montana town set on a ridge overlooking Beaver Creek Basin.

Maybe the idea of taking up a homestead had been sort of loco for a cowpuncher. Well, Bootjack had claimed so, but a man has to settle down some time, doesn't he?

Or does he?

Anyway, here he was—an enemy of Big Ike Outland's, and maybe he should be Big Ike's friend, if he wanted to find out what had become of Rusty and about three thousand head of Texas cattle. He poured the drinks around again and pondered momentarily on the turn of events. The summer before Rusty Carlin had left Texas with a small herd of U U cattle, looking for range in Montana. Time had gone by and Jim had waited for word from his brother but that word never came.

Jim and Bootjack James would have headed north with Rusty except for the fact that they had been serving time on a Texas chain gang making little rocks out of big ones, the result of too much youth and gunplay when they had shot up a dinky Texas burg, just to watch the citizens dig their holes. So Rusty and old

Pancho Torres, an old Mexican, had headed out alone, with Jim and Bootjack aiming to catch up with them if they could break camp, or after their sentences were served.

"Another round, men?"

"Sure thing, stranger."

Jim poured drinks again. And again the loafers downed their shots with great ease. The bartender started to get out of his chair and Bootjack turned suddenly and the bartender sank back down again.

Jim said, "That's killin' that Injun, Bootjack."

"Whiskey'll kill him."

The drinkers stared at them. Apparently some of them were beginning to show great misgivings as to the sanity of this strange pair. Here they were talking about killing an Indian and there wasn't even an Indian in the saloon.

One edged away from Jim.

Jim saw this and almost smiled. But he managed to keep a straight face.

"He's done quit beatin' his tom-tom, Bootjack."

"Is he a Sioux or a Cheyenne?"

Jim shook his head. "Gros Ventres," he corrected. "Another drink, friends?"

But the loafers had had enough. One by one they declined the kind offer and Jim knew the reason why—they figured that he and Bootjack were slightly *tetched in the haid*.

By the time Jim had downed his slug the last of the loafers had slipped through the door into the sunshine outside.

"How much we owe you, barkeeper?"

The man stated his sum. Jim solemnly paid him and thanked him. By this time the man had lost his grouch. He had a drink with them and put it on the house. He had back his natural good humor.

"Gosh danged it, men, but I sure got took over the coals. Well, it's my fault; but when Big Ike got word you two had drifted out onto Hell Crick, he sent out word for me not to let a nester drink here."

"He kinda runs this burg, eh?" Jim wanted to know.

"Sorta."

Bootjack made his hands open and close. Jim noticed that the bartender kept a comfortable distance. He got the impression that much of the man's good-humor was plainly forced. The bartender figured he was catering to two crazy men. Jim turned his glass slowly and looked at the ring it made.

"You know," he said, "I never did get to file on my homestead."

"That's right," Bootjack said.

Jim felt gingerly of his head. "I owe that clerk a visit," he opined. "How about it, Bootjack?"

"We owe him a visit, Jim."

3

THE clerk had a black eye. Jim said, "Your right one is black an' my left one is black. Ain't no justice, is there!"

The clerk was suspicious. "Maybe they ain't; maybe they is. What do you want? Ain't you done enough damage? If 'n the sheriff had been in town he'd a-stopped you right pronto."

"But he ain't in town," Jim said. "I want to finish filin' for my homestead."

"Are you completely crazy? Big Ike Outland will pick you to pieces!"

"He didn't, did he?"

"No, but—"

Jim said. "You work for the county and the gover'ment, I'd judge, seein' you're the county clerk an' also the land agent. By law I have a right to file on Hell Crick. Trot out your forms and I'll put my John Henry on them."

The clerk shrugged. "Your funeral."

They made out the necessary forms. Within a week, the clerk said, the surveyor would drive out and make a survey and establish corner posts. Where was the surveyor now? Over to Great Falls for a meeting.

"Prob'ly drunk," Bootjack murmured.

"The surveyor, sir, is a non-drinker." The clerk spoke to Jim. "The fee is two dollars, sir."

Jim said, "We ain't through yet. We just filed papers for a farming homestead of a hundred and sixty acres. I'm aimin' to file a grazing claim, a timber claim, and I want water rights to Hell Crick."

"Sir, that's a lot of land."

"Mebbe so but trot out your papers."

The clerk scowled and went to his file drawer. Jim winked at Bootjack who winked back. The clerk had deliberately made out the first claim for a farming-homestead only; evidently he had figured Jim so ignorant that he did not know about the other filing-claims.

Janet Albers came in.

"Howdy, deputy," Jim said.

"What's this I hear about you havin' a ruckus in the saloon?" she asked impatiently.

Jim looked at Bootjack. "She goes right to the point, eh?" He spoke to the blonde girl. "Honey, you've got it all wrong; we did not create a disturbance. Honey, that saloon was plumb peaceful when we was in there. Ain't that right, Bootjack?"

"Shorely is, pal."

China-blue eyes switched one to the other. "The bartender said you choked him, Mr. Bootjack."

"Why, shucks, ma'am, I shore can't understand that, I can't. We had a peaceful little chat; I shore can't understan' why he claims that."

China-blue eyes went back to Jim. "Somebody must be crazy, and I don't believe it's me. I ought to jug both of you buckos for disturbing the peace."

"Now that sure ain't a nice way to greet friends," Jim lamented.

The clerk came back with some more forms. He was sour and melancholy. His pen moved laboriously, scratching like a hen digging in gravel, and his fingers were stiff as icicles.

"Still aiming on taking up land on Hell Crick?" the girl wanted to know.

Jim nodded.

"Just stay out of trouble," Janet Albers warned.

She went out, back straight. Jim looked at Bootjack and smiled, but the big man had a straight face.

"She might've jugged us, Jim."

"I'd've talked her out of it."

Bootjack shook his head. "I got a sudden mind she's got a brain of her own, an' a will to match it."

Jim said to the clerk, "All through?"

"All through. You sign there."

The clerk had his nose close to the paper for evidently his eyes were none too good. Jim had a dull headache; the clerk had given it to him. He signed and then he reached across the counter and got the clerk before he could get out of reach. He struggled with him and then he got his nose into the ink-well. The clerk kicked and started to holler and Jim stuck a wet blotter in his mouth. When the clerk got his head back up his nose and mouth were dripping with ink.

"The Law'll git you for this!"

Jim shook his head. He vaulted the counter, ran the clerk down and caught him behind a desk. He carried the struggling, kicking man toward a door that evidently led to a side room. Bootjack had the door open. Jim pitched the clerk ahead without looking into the room.

"Lord," Bootjack breathed. "That weren't no room, Jim. You done heaved him plumb down a cellar."

"Listen to him thud down the steps."

Bootjack looked in. "He's down there in a heap. Kinda dark down there. Naw, he ain't dead; he moved."

"He'll come out of it."

"What if you kilt him?"

"Me kill him?" Jim showed surprise. "Why, how could I kill him? He went to go down the stairs and he tripped and fell. You an' me weren't even in the room, we weren't."

"He'll tell the truth."

"An' we'll lie like hades. Our two words against his one. We're gettin' nowhere in a terrible haste."

"Sure looks like it."

Jim pocketed his forms and they went outside. Jim said, "You know, my head has almost stopped achin'."

To this Bootjack James had no reply. His face, Jim noticed, was rather serious; the blue-shaven jowls hung dejectedly, the black eyes held no snap. Evidently his partner was worried about the short period of time they had spent in Beaver Tail town.

"Look, Jim."

Big Ike Outland and Toad Graham had just come out of a log building. Jim noticed a sign that said, *Henry J. Kingman, MD.*, over the building's door. To get to their horses he and Bootjack would meet the two cowmen.

Bootjack murmured, "Let's try to keep away from trouble, Jim."

Jim nodded. "You wanta remember that Big Ike clipped me first."

Big Ike and Toad stood and stared at them. Big Ike Outland looked like a harrow and a disc had run over his face. Toad Graham chewed tobacco and swung his head slowly back and forth like a bull does in nosefly time.

"Wait a minute," Big Ike clipped.

Jim Carlin and Bootjack James stopped.

"How about that homestead you aimed to take up, Carlin?"

Jim smiled. "Got the papers in my pocket, chief. When I get done I'll own almost a section of that Hell Crick range. A little bird done tol' me you run the O Bar O Connected iron north of here."

"He chirped rightly, Carlin. An' if you got the sense of a halfbaked jackass you'd jes' keep ridin' right on."

Jim looked at Bootjack. "Now who the heck would bake a jackass, Bootjack?"

"I dunno."

Toad said nothing. He just studied Bootjack like an executioner studies his next victim. His eyes were the flat unblinking eyes of a toad. He seemed very much interested in Bootjack's enormous hands.

"You ever break a man's neck with them hands?" Toad wanted to know.

Bootjack lied with, "Sure have, gent. An' be danged careful or I might lose my temper an' snap your neck in two."

Toad said nothing. He blinked and stopped chewing. He seemed to be considering Bootjack's statement seriously. Then his gaze became fixed again and his jaw started working. But he was still silent.

Janet Albers came out of the courthouse and stopped about twenty feet away, just close enough to listen to their conversation. Jim Carlin noticed that she packed a double-barrel saw-down shot-gun. He knew darned well it wasn't empty, either.

"Big Ike, I never come on this range lookin' for trouble, savvy. I come here to settle down in peace. You're afraid if I settle down an' farm then other sodbusters will come in an' squat on your grass. You know, I'm a waddy myself; Texas way, I come from—an' I might play out pushin' a plow, savvy?"

"Which all leads to what?"

"Well, mebbe so I might not farm, at that. I'll put it to you frankly. I ain't got much dinero an' my partner has less. If we did get some crop in it wouldn't be until next fall that we'd have some dinero an' that's over a year off."

"That's your neck."

Toad watched, eyes set. Occasionally he clenched and unclenched his hands. He watched Bootjack James.

"It leads up to this. Me an' my pard might need jobs a punchin' dogies an '—"

"You get no jobs on the O Bar O Connected!"

Jim tried another tactic. "You jumped me, fella, an' don't fergit that. If you'd've gone about it peaceful we might not have had no trouble. But if I ever catch you or this human bullfrog on this spread I'm filin' on I'll shoot both of you so full of holes you'll leak for the rest of your lives!"

"No trouble," Janet Albers warned.

Jim smiled at her. "You sure are a purty little honey, Miss Albers." He looked back at Big Ike. "I offer a white flag an' you turned it down, Big Ike. If you want war then war it is."

Toad blinked, then resumed his staring.

"Get out of town," Janet Albers ordered.

She raised the shotgun a trifle.

Bootjack spoke hurriedly. "Jim, let's vamoose! I don't trust that heifer as far as I could kick a stud horse."

Jim looked at her thumb. It was easing back the hammer of the right-hand barrel. "Neither do I," he concurred.

4

JIM and Bootjack had raised so much turmoil in Beaver Tail that evidently nobody had noticed the two riders who had ridden up and rein-tied their broncs in front of the courthouse. It was only when Jim and his parner were mounted that both came out of the courthouse on the run and slammed into their saddles.

Bootjack gasped, hardly believing his eyes, "Hell, they're masked, Jim! They've held up the courthouse!"

A man ran out of the courthouse. "Holdup! Holdup!" His screech was metallic.

Beaver Tail town came wide awake. People came out of the few business establishments and somebody ran out with a shotgun. Already the bandits were making their escape, their broncs kicking up dust and gravel. The shotgun boomed but the outlaws were too far away.

The two bore down on Jim and Bootjack, who sat their broncs in the road. Jim said, "My Gawd, Bootjack, they're comin' right down on us—an' our guns are in leather!"

"Up goes my paws, Jim!"

Jim raised his hands, too. Both of the bandits held sixshooters and to try to fight it out with them would be suicide. They came toward them with spurs working, with dust behind them. Through the dust Jim glimpsed Janet Albers running out of the Mercantile. She brought her shotgun up and let both barrels go. The heavy jolt almost knocked her down. A sixshooter lead sang over Jim's head.

Jim hollered, "Count us out!" and spurred his horse up on the plank sidewalk. Bootjack followed suit.

"Good boys!"

The closest bandit, about forty feet away, snarled the words. Jim got a good look at his horse. He was a buckskin with a lineback—a powerful, long-legged bronc that showed a touch of thoroughbred in the way he dug out and ran. Jim saw that tar had been smeared over the horse's right shoulder to hide his brand. He couldn't see the man's face because of the black mask. But the wind had blown back the man's hat until it hung from the jawstrap against his back. And Jim saw flaming red hair.

He did not have time to glance at the other rider. For they were gone then, slanting their broncs around a corner of a building.

Jim stared at Bootjack. The man's eyes were heavy with something that looked like surprise.

"Jim, did I see rightly?"

Jim murmured, "Lord, I hope we're both wrong. There's more than one waddy that's got hair that red, I reckon."

"But the horse he rode, Jim! That was ol' Sonny, sure as I'm a foot—Jim it can't be true."

"I hope not," Jim repeated.

Bootjack's big face was the picture of acute mental suffering. "That was Sonny,

Jim; I'd know that big buckskin anywhere. And that tar smeared on him could hide a U U brand, 'cause that's where Sonny packs the iron—right on his right shoulder. That was Rusty, sure as hell."

Jim said, "I feel sick, friend."

"So do I."

Men were running for horses. Townsmen hairpinned into saddles and waved rifles and sixshooters. A man came running out of the courthouse. Jim and Bootjack heard his bellowed words.

"They got around ten thousand, people! Somebody done throwed the clerk down the cellar an' he's out cold an' the safe is wide open. Every cent this town has got is in their saddlebags!"

"And the sheriff is out of town, too, when he should be tendin' to his duties. Come on, citizens."

Jim said, "By the time that would-be posse gets goin' them bandits'll be in Canady. Boy alive, look at that Janet woman ride that hoss! Sets that saddle like she's a part of it—"

Janet's bronc was rearing. He walked on his hind legs. Jim saw the girl brandishing a rifle.

"Follow me, men!"

They galloped down the street. Jim and Bootjack still had their broncs on the sidewalk. Jim growled, "Man, this town *is* a hoodoo, like you said. When that clerk comes to an' tells that we heaved him down them stairs these people'll think for sure we was in cahoots with these bandits, workin' from inside!"

"Holy smoke, I never thought of that."

"We ride with this posse, savvy."

Janet Albers hollered, "You men ride with us, savvy?" and Jim spurred his bronc even with hers. The big bartender put his horse up with them. "Why the heck didn't you shoot at them, stranger? They rode right past you!"

"Yeah, an' their guns was drawed too, fella! I don't crave to commit suicide."

"One of them had his hat blowed off. Did you know him?"

Jim said, "He had a mask on."

"This way," Janet said.

The bartender fell back. Jim glanced and counted heads—about sixteen men. Toad and Big Ike rode with the posse. Big Ike roweled his horse ahead and shouted orders.

"They'll be headin' toward the Big Muddy, men. They've got quite a start on us, but we may have a chance."

"They got somethin' else beside a good start," a fat man grumbled. "They got about three odd thousan' of my dinero, they have!"

"With them high prices you have in your store, Clem, you'll get thet all back in a week," a cowpuncher shouted.

The Big Muddy—the common name for the Missouri River—was about fifty miles to the south. They raced across the creek bottom toward the sandrock-dotted hills to the south, about three miles away.

"There they go into the hills, men!"

Jim saw the two riders, then—they were loping into the hills, which reared high and ugly. Once in that sanctuary they were more or less safe. Again he glimpsed buckskin horse, and then the riders were in the hills.

Bootjack said, "We could never run them out of there."

Jim nodded. After all, he and Bootjack had lost nothing in the holdup. He felt a tight knot in the region of his belly. This sight of the buckskin with the tar-smeared brand—the sight of the flaming red hair on that bandit—they had put the knot there. And now his thoughts were pulling the strands even tighter . . .

But, looking back, he realized, now more than ever, that Rusty Carlin always had been a wild one, even down in Texas. Still, Rusty was his brother, and blood is blood.

Jim knew the posse could never hope to catch the pair. Two men with Winchesters could drop from their broncs, settle behind rocks, and cut the posse members loose from their saddles with well-placed bullets.

"Spread out," he hollered.

"I'm runnin' this," Big Ike reminded loudly.

"You'll run us right into lead," Jim growled. "Thet pair'll hole up an' we'll ride smack into a trap, maybe."

"They'll run," Big Ike grunted. "C'yotees like them two is always run afore they fight. They're part of that Larb Crick bunch, I'll say."

Jim didn't know anything about the "Larb Crick bunch." He knew that Larb Creek came into Beaver Creek right above the town of Beaver Tail and he knew it flowed in from the south and had its source in the Larb Hills. But he did know he didn't aim to ride into an ambush.

He pulled in his bronc.

"I'm not ridin' into an ambush," he stated. "Big Ike, if you're so dumb, you ride into it."

"He's right," a townsman said.

Another man said, "Hell, we cain't catch them, anyway. They got too big a start. Them's the same two gents what stuck up the Malta bank last month. One of them men rode a buckskin, too."

"The same pair," Big Ike said. He scanned the hills. "I hate to see them get away. They're takin' all the money out of Beaver Tail. Everyone of us had our money stored in the clerk's safe. He was the town banker an' I hope he didn't get hurt too bad."

Jim suddenly remembered the thud the clerk had made when he had hit the bottom of the cellar. He knew he and Bootjack had worked themselves into a tough situation. The clerk would claim they were part of the bandit gang and their job had been to get him out of circulation.

Jim glanced anxiously at Bootjack. The big man's thumb made a significant gesture that silently said, "Mister, we'd better dust out of here pronto." And Jim nodded.

Everything had gone haywire. They had got into trouble with Toad Graham and Big Ike Outland and then they had carried their act just a little bit too far—and now it had backfired on them. And backfired with a whale of a bang.

Coincidence had come in, also. Now why had those two bandits taken that particular day—and a time when they had the town of Beaver Tail literally standing on its head—to hit at the clerk's office and make off with the local bankroll?

Jim was worried, and his grin was ironical. Deputy Sheriff Janet Albers was close to tears of frustration and disappointment and she saw the grin.

"What are you smiling about, you wild jackass?"

"It amuses me how dumb Big Ike is. This posse should split up into pairs and go into the hills—anything to keep from being in a bunch thisaway—"

"So I'm dumb, eh?" Big Ike Outland had reined his sweaty horse close to Jim's. His face was the color of a bloodbay horse and a vein stood out on his neck like a hemp rope. "Climb off 'n that hoss, cowboy, an' repeat that statement?"

"With pleasure."

Before either could dismount townsmen had spurred between them. Jim was glad for the interference. He knew he could never beat any brains into Big Ike's dumb skull.

"No fightin' men!"

Janet said, "This man has a good idea. Split up into pairs, and take to the hills. Big Ike, you ride with me."

Big Ike was suddenly smiling. "With pleasure, Miss Janet."

"You ride with us too, Toad."

Toad smiled now. "With great pleasure."

Jim glanced at Big Ike. The cowman's smile had gone and the O Bar O Connected owner was scowling with displeasure.

"Ride out, men," Janet ordered.

Jim's plan had worked. By this ruse he and Bootjack could separate from the posse without any suspicions.

An hour later he and his partner sat on the sandstones that overlooked the homestead on Hell Creek.

5

JIM said, "We sure got balled up, pard."

Bootjack chewed on a dried blade of foxtail. "Well, we sure did, Jim." He summed it all up. "We're on thet chain-gang an' Rusty an' Pancho head north with three thousand head of dogies. We busts out to go with them an' the Law nabs us an' adds time onto our sentence."

"Why bring that up?"

"I wanta git a complete picture of this. Come spring we head out for Montana, an we' still ain't got no word from either Rusty or Pancho. We fin' out the trailherd crossed the Missouri River south of here an' then the whul trail just sags in an' is lost."

Jim remembered the red-headed bandit. "Until today," he corrected.

"Maybe thet wasn't Rusty."

Jim shrugged. "We can hope."

"Well, here we is, an' here is a gent named Big Ike who runs the O Bar O Connected iron. We both know cow brands. Our trailherd was branded U U. Get a hot runnin' iron an' make the two U's into O's by completin' the loop over the top of them, like this."

Bootjack's dirty finger made grooves in the dust.

"Then add a bar between them an' what do you have?" He answered his own question. O Bar O Connected. Like this: O-O."

"On the right ribs, too," Jim said.

Bootjack said, "We could shoot down a cow that totes the O Bar O Connected, an' we could scrape the hide from the inside. If the brand was originally the U U we could tell that-away."

Jim nodded.

Bootjack chewed on his blade of grass. Up the gulch a magpie sat in a stunted service-berry tree and made ugly noises. His raucous voice came to them and then echoed from the rocks.

"Might've been Rusty," Bootjack said at length.

"Might've been," Jim agreed.

Bootjack spat out his blade of grass. "Damn it all, Jim wouldn't it break a man's heart, though. I cain't hardly believe that Rusty would swing out onto the hootowl trail, but come to think of it he always was kinda bull-haided an' wild, like the time he wrapped his twine onto the bars in thet Texas jail an' pulled them out like roots an' all to get a pal out of the clink."

"We'd've done the same had we been in a like situation."

Bootjack looked squarely at him. "You figger thet bandit was Rusty?"

Jim pointed out that the man had Rusty's build and red hair and he rode Sonny.

"The gent was masked but Sonny sure wasn't, an' I'd know that pony any place —shucks, I was the first to lay a saddle on him, if you remember . . ."

"Might have been somebody else astraddle him, Jim."

"Might have been," Jim allowed; "Still, I'd bet my last buck the rider was Rusty."

Bootjack digested that with a serious, heavy face. Finally he said, "Well, we know one thing: Rusty is still alive. He looked plumb at us an' I'll bet he was su'prised. He'll swing aroun' an' look us up, I figger."

"I think so."

"You don't sound very happy."

Jim Carlin groaned aloud. "How could I be happy? Here we send my kid brother north with all our cattle because Texas has no more open range an' we want to run cows in Montana. We don't hear from him an' you is in the clink jes' because a town marshal got a little peeved with us."

"You shot a hole in his hat."

"That wasn't a serious offense. I didn't shoot a hole in his head an' I could have just as easy as ventilatin' his hat."

Down the gulch the magpie suddenly stopped scolding.

"A rider comin'," Jim said.

They couldn't see the rider but they

could hear his bronc's hoofs sound occasionally on the igneous bed of the canyon, for the horse was steel-shod. The hoof-noise stopped, and the partners listened; about five minutes later, the sound started again.

"Scoutin' aroun'," Jim murmured. "He's cut our trail but he loses it now an' then because of them flinty rocks."

"Somebody trailin' us, eh? Now who could that be?"

"Might be Big Ike or Toad. Or it might be that that clerk got out to see Janet Albers an' she's sent word out to pick us up."

"Could be both of them reasons, Jim."

Jim said, "Split up, leave our broncs hid here, an' we'll scout back."

"I'll take this side of the canyon."

Jim nodded. He took the east slope of the canyon. The soil was thick with boulders, and the mulberry trees and serviceberry trees made progress difficult. Wild rosebushes had plenty of thorns, too. Occasionally he stopped and listened and at these moments his lanky body lost its tension and a strange form of heartsickness touched him when he remembered the bandit with the flaming red hair. He only hoped that the man had not been Rusty. But he knew the horse had been Sonny, and he felt sure the bandit was his brother.

Discouragement, mingled with anger, had touched him when he had discovered that Rusty and old Pancho and the U U trailherd had so miraculously disappeared this side of the Big Muddy. Discouragement because his plan to settle down and become a peaceful rancher had suddenly dissolved into thin air; anger because he felt sure that Rusty and the Mexican had fallen victims of foul play—and this anger had been directed toward the unknown person or persons responsible for this foul play. But the sight of Sonny—and the red-headed rider—

It had, to put it mildly, stunned him.

Squatting, he listened.

The magpie was silent. He flew overhead—a gaudy, black-and-white bird. He was flying toward the direction where, but a few moments before, Jim and Bootjack had been. That meant that the rider was coming up the canyon.

Jim heard the horse, and the sound came from the bed of the canyon; this was about a hundred feet way. The horse stopped. Jim peered through the brush. The rider was down on one knee, still holding his bridle reins, and he scanned the soil, plainly looking for fresh tracks.

Jim saw a man who was as skinny as a lodgepole pine. He wore tub-faded levis and run-over boots and a flannel shirt and an old vest. He turned slightly and Jim saw a face that was as long as that of a lonesome hound dog. A weather-tanned face, rough as old rawhide.

He also saw something else, too. The man toted a lawstar on his open vest. Jim thought, "Sheriff Albers, sure as shootin'."

Now what the heck was Albers doing in this canyon?

There was only one answer. The sheriff had met the posse and evidently word had got out from Beaver Tail about Jim and

Bootjack throwing the county-clerk down the stairway. Therefore, Sheriff Albers had headed out to trail down both Jim and Bootjack. Down in town he had heard that the Sheriff liked to work alone.

He had also got a short description of the sheriff, who had been over to the neighboring county-seat on official business, he had heard. And this man fitted Albers' description.

The sheriff stood up and looked about him, eyes squinted. Jim knew that he would follow the trail right on to where his horse and the bronc of Bootjack were hidden. He wished he could get word to Bootjack to pull out. Once on their cayuses they could duck away but on foot—

Suddenly the lanky man said, "Come out of that brush, fellow, an' come out with them paws of your'n up high!"

Jim thought that the lawman had seen him, but he was mistaken. The lawman had his back to him and was facing the buckbrush on the other side of the coulee. He had his gun level and demanding.

"Come on out, an' keep them hands up."

Bootjack James walked out of the brush, hands even with his shoulders. Jim prided himself on having good ears but he realized that this lawman had him skinned in the hearing department. He had not heard a sound that would have indicated that Bootjack had been in that particular clump of buckbrush.

"I'm Sheriff Mike Albers. You the gent they call Bootjack James?"

"I might be, an' I might not be!"

Jim noticed that Bootjack's wide face sported a very dejected look.

"I ran into my posse back yonder when I was cuttin' over from Dawson City, an' my girl tol' me about you two an' the hell you raised down in Beaver Tail, an' then I meets the county clerk—"

Jim thought, "You can stop right there, fella, 'cause we can guess the rest."

"Where's your pard?" Albers demanded.

Jim grunted to himself, "Here," and he left the brush silently. He crossed the strip of sand and then hit the igneous canyon bottom and the sheriff heard his boots. Albers tried to turn.

"Look out fer his gun, Jim!"

Bootjack's words were wasted. Sheriff Mike Albers lurched ahead thrown off-stride by Jim's tackling lunge. Sheriff Albers shouted, "I'm the Law, damnit, an' you'll suffer fer this—!" and Jim's impact pounded the breath from the lawman. The star toter's .45 went off but the lead went harmlessly skyward. By this time Jim had the .45 by the barrel. A quick wrench and he had brought the sheriff's arm up and back, and Albers screamed in pain for Jim was hammer-locking his right arm. The .45 spun out to land in the sand; Albers jerked loose.

"I'll git him!"

Big Bootjack wanted a chance to redeem himself, and he did. His right came out and connected head-on with Sheriff Mike Albers' thin jaw. The sheriff sighed and went down.

Jim panted, "Maybe you broke his

neck! You handed him an awful blow, man!"

Bootjack paled. He knelt and wobbled Albers' limp neck. He lowered his head down to the man's chest.

"Nah, he ain't dead. He's jes' sleepin'."

Albers' mouth slackened and opened.

"Maybe you busted his jaw?"

Bootjack tested the man's jaw by wiggling it. "Nah, h'ain't busted, Jim. Say, things look frothy for us, eh?"

Jim nodded. "Whole damned deal done backfired. Well, we'd best get out of here pronto, 'cause when this gent comes to there'll be warrants out for us boys. Us for our cayuses."

"There'll be warrants filed," Bootjack substantiated.

They ran to the spot where they had hidden their broncs. They swung up and rode down Hell Creek and across the land on which Jim had just filed first-papers. They had four extra horses and a pack mule and these were grazing in the grass along the lazy creek.

Jim said, "We leave them there. They won't stray far; they're too tired from the long trip."

"What's our plan?"

Jim told his partner what he aimed to do.

6

FROM a high vantage point, way up in the sandstones that made up the rimrock cap, Jim and Bootjack watched Sheriff Mike Albers point his pony toward the town of Beaver Tail. The sheriff must have been unconscious for quite a spell because it was an hour or so before he came riding out of the buck-brush in the canyon.

"Bet he's got a headache," Bootjack opined.

Jim grunted, "We'll have headaches if the law catches us."

"Things has gone against us."

Jim nodded. "Get a ca'tridge in your rifle, pard."

Bootjack pulled his Winchester from its saddle-scabbard. The breech made a sliding click as the big man tested the barrel to see if a cartridge was nestled in it.

"Done loaded, Jim."

Jim rose on stirrups and pointed toward a rise ahead. The summit of it was topped with a scatteration of gnarled boxelder trees and buckbrush.

"Yonder's some cows, boy."

They turned out to be Big Ike Outland's O Bar O Connected cattle. The U U herd had consisted of mostly cows and calves for a man cannot start a cow-outfit by driving up only steers from Texas.

Jim said, "How about that old brockle-faced bossy over there?"

"She's the one."

Bootjack's .30–30 made a sharp crack. The cow stopped chewing her cud. Her knees broke and she went down.

"I hated to do that," Bootjack said quietly.

Jim nodded.

They skinned the cow and laid the hide on the soil. They got a flat rock under the section that had the brand and they scraped the hide carefully with their jack-nives. When a brand is worked over with a hot running-iron there can usually be found traces of the old brand when the hide is fleshed. That is because the old iron has already made a scar tissue and the new burn does not affect this as it does fresh hide. They scraped and looked and when they had finished the dusk was thick.

Jim said, "That cow died for nothin'."

Bootjack nodded. "No trace of an old brand. And by gosh, Jim, it seems to me that was one of our cows from Texas; if she weren't she sure looked like one that went into that trailherd."

Jim sat down on a boulder and cleaned his pocket-knife in some dried grass. "You watch the homestead," he said. "If that red-headed bugger really was Rusty, then he might come down there an' look for me."

"You watch yourself."

"You do likewise, pal."

They didn't shake hands. Jim swung up and rode toward the south. Bootjack got his saddle under him and he rode downslope toward Hell Creek. Jim lost sight of the big man and then looked south. The posse was still out hunting for the gents who had robbed the county clerk's office and if the posse ran into him it would be mighty bad for him. He didn't want to get behind bars again.

He didn't like lattice-work in front of his bed.

Twilight changed to early night and Jim was in the badlands, then. This was a land of erosion, a land of twisted buttes and crooked spires cut by Nature's rain and wind. Jim kept pointing his horse south. But he was not without vigilance; many times he stopped, dismounted, hidden by buckbrush. One time Big Ike Outland rode about fifty feet from him totally unaware of Jim's hiding-place. Jim noticed that the owner of the O-O Connected was riding southward. That seemed a little out of reason. The O Bar O Connected was to the southwest, mostly west. Jim waited until the man had passed and then swung in behind him a safe distance, but he lost the heavy man somewhere in the night. He did not ride all night. He made a camp in the rocks but he did not dare light a fire. He lay back against a boulder and let his pony graze on his picket. He felt lonesome and as lost as he had ever felt when a child. He did not feel lost because he was in strange surroundings; he felt lost because he remembered a bandit swinging a gun on him—a bandit with red hair, a bandit who rode a buckskin bronc with a pitch-smeared brand.

He dozed.

Dawn came with a cold wind. He found himself wishing that he had had time to settle down on his homestead—that this hadn't happened so he could be sleeping behind thick log walls that turned the cold Montana wind. But he was still on edge and he was squatting in thick brush when Janet Albers rode by. She was pointing her pony north toward Beaver Tail town.

Jim felt a little surprise. She was at least twenty-five miles from town, she was alone despite the fact she was only a woman, and she evidently had been out all night. In the light of the dawn he could see her face. She looked tired and bedraggled—which was unusual for Janet Albers. Every time that Jim had seen her he had thought her more beautiful than the last—and, while she looked beautiful even now, her eyes lacked their vivacious twinkle, her shoulders were bowed as though she had been carrying around a physical burden rather than a mental one. *What's she been up to?* Jim asked himself —but he knew that the answer would have to eventually come from the beautifully-shaped lips of the lovely Deputy Sheriff.

He stepped out, gun in hand.

"Who the heck—?"

He grinned. "A little boy named Jim Carlin, Miss Janet."

She stared at him. "Why, my father went over to your homestead, and I figured for sure he had you in jail by now."

"Never seen hide nor hair of him," Jim lied.

She looked at his gun. Evidently she

did not fear him, for Jim could read no fear in her face; rather, she seemed angry with herself for letting him surprise her this way.

"You get home early," Jim commented.

She stormed, "You put that gun away, Jim Carlin!"

He shook his head slowly. "You're a purty young woman, Miss Janet, but that little finger of yours can squeeze a trigger, even though you are purty. You an' the rest of this range figger that me an' my pard was in on that holdup. To tell you that I wasn't would only make you call me a liar."

"You must have been the inside men! Word came that you threw the clerk down the cellar stairs and laid him out. You made a pretense of riding with my posse and then you sneaked away like the miserable hound-dog that you are!"

"You're full of compliments," Jim said.

He smiled but it was not a pleasant smile. For a man doesn't show a pleasant face when a beautiful young woman bawls him out.

"You find any of them bandits, ma'am?"

"I didn't, and I pounded leather all night. They reached the Larb Hills, I guess. You seem to be headed that way, I take it."

Jim said, "I'm leavin' the country. Neither me or my pard was in on that holdup, although you claim otherwise. We jes' ran smack-dab into some bad luck but neither of us has ever bin crowded by good luck very danged far."

"There'll be placards and a warrant out for you."

Jim shrugged. "So there'll have to be." He went forward. "Ma'am, I'll have to trouble you for your rifle and your short-gun. I'll leave them about a mile ahead on the trail in a spot where you can find them easy-like but jes' now I don't crave lead through me when I ride away."

"You don't take my word?"

Jim said, "You tote a star, purty girl."

She reached for her holstered gun. Her

face was flushed and anger made her bite her bottom lip.

"Jus' a minute!"

Her hand stopped.

"What?"

"Don't draw that gun. Get off your bronc an' turn your back to me an' I'll take it from your holster."

She started to dismount. To do so her horse would be between Jim and her.

"No, this side. The right side."

"I'm no Indian and this is no Indian pony."

"He won't buck if you get off the wrong side."

"I'll try."

Her horse, although tired, was skittish; he didn't want his rider mounting and dismounting from the right side. But she got her boots on the ground and Jim came in behind her, holstering his own gun. Before he could get her pistol she had turned and grabbed for his gun. He jumped to one side and she went ahead, almost falling, but he caught her.

She was soft and warm, and Jim had

been a long, long time away from a woman. She was close to him and she smelled clean and healthy; her lips were parted slightly. Jim knew he shouldn't have done it but he held her close and kissed her. She said, "Let go of me, damn you!" and she hit him in the face. He grinned and kissed her again and she struck again and then she quit fighting. She became meek and had no resistance; Jim stepped back, a little ashamed of himself.

"Have you had your little fun?" Her voice was cutting in its sarcasm.

"It seems to me," Jim said slowly, "that you answered one of my kisses."

She blushed then. He had hit home, he realized.

"Sir, it is your imagination, I assure you, and nothing more."

Jim had her .45. He slipped her Winchester out of its saddle-holster.

She said, 'You still don't trust me?"

"You still tote a star."

She smiled, but her smile was forced. "Maybe I should throw it away?"

Jim said, "That's your business."

"Maybe," she said, "I'll see you again . . . soon?"

Jim did smile this time. "You're not much at the task you're trying to do Miss Janet. You're too honest an' clean, I guess. I'm sorry that I grabbed you like that, and I want you to believe it. If I ever come and see you it'll be when I'm not wanted by your father. I've had a few run-ins with the Law but it came about because I was young an' full of hell. Them days is gone—now I'm only full of hell! Savvy?"

"You go to hell," she stormed.

Jim was serious. "Mebbe so I'm a-headin' that way, ma'am. Anyway, I want to leave this with you, please: I am not in on this holdup nor was my partner in on it—we're like the man says, 'Just victims of circumstance'."

"It doesn't look that way to me or the people on this range!"

Jim bowed a little very courteously. "I'm sorry to hear you say that, Miss Janet." His daredevilry returned and showed in his smile. "Now I'd best git out of here or I'll be plumb tempted to kiss you again."

She bit her lip but said nothing.

He left her standing there. Once over the hill he put spurs to his mount and rode south. She didn't know it but in the tussle he had stolen her law badge. He put his hand in his pocket and fingered the badge.

A funny world, an odd world, he mused.

He liked the feel of that badge.

Someday he'd walk up to Janet and say, "Here's a little trophy I want you to have. You lost it in a canyon . . . remember?"

And he'd hand her the badge.

But where he was going toting a lawbadge was a dangerous habit. He decided he would cache the badge back in the rocks. He hid it under a loose boulder and then rode on toward Larb City. The country grew rougher and stunted timber took the place of buck-brush. Gnarled scrub pine bent in front of the wind. Then he came to a mesa and Larb City was ahead.

Would he find Rusty there in this longrider hangout?

7

LARB CITY had once been a line-camp site for a horse-outfit. But horses had not paid off in hard cash so the owner had turned his spread into a rustler camp, so Jim heard. From stealing cattle the outfit spread out and became proficient in other forms of thievery—one of these forms consisted of sticking-up trains and banks. Or so Dame Rumor claimed . . .

The original owner of the site, he had heard, was dead from too much weight on his legs—a tough case had weighted him down with too much lead. But Jim wasn't interested in the past history of the place; he was interested in only one thing —had Rusty gone outlaw and would he find him here in this camp?

The scatteration of tin shacks and tarpaper roofs was not a pleasant sight in the rawness of the cold wind, for heavy clouds scuttled across the sky as if in a hurry to reach Dakota Territory to the east. A bony hound dog came out snapped at the heels of Jim's bronc. The cowpuncher's lass-rope made a sharp crack, the free end wrapped itself cuttingly around the hound's gaunt middle, and the dog limped toward a sod shack, whimpering in pain.

"You all quit beatin' mah dog!"

The words came from a slatternly hag who toted a broom. The wind whipped her dirty dress against her lean shanks.

"You all quit siccin' your dog onto me," Jim drawled.

She cursed him, waving the broom at him. Jim found what he considered was a livery-barn, although it did not carry a sign, and he rode into its wide front door, glad to be out of the raw wind.

"Grain him, fella, an' feed him right royal."

Aged eyes appraised Jim's bronc. "Looks like he's bin rid right smart an' right sudden, too."

"That's my business," Jim clipped.

He threw the old man a dollar and went out on the dirt sidewalk. He walked between two swayback buildings and watched the sidewalk. Soon the old hostler hustled by, heading for the local saloon. Jim moved around and entered the livery-barn by its back door.

The place was filled with horses, it seemed; only two stalls were empty. Jim walked along the runway and looked them over but he saw no buckskin tied to the manger. He glanced at brands and found them all alien: Quarter Circle S D, N Bar 9, the Smokestack, Circle 8, and others.

He did not go out the front door. He went out the back door and returned up the alley. On the street he stopped and gave this burg—such as it was—a slow scrutiny. His eyes finally settled on the Pine Tree Saloon, directly across the street. He saw the half-awning over the window suddenly rustle. He knew that eyes had been watching him.

He turned suddenly and looked toward the store. A man hurriedly jerked his head back but Jim saw him through the dirty window.

"Being watched," he thought.

He heard the rap-rap of high heels and he turned. She was a woman of about twenty-five, he figured; her hips were full and so were her breasts, and her dress showed both to a good advantage.

"Honey," she said, "you must be chilly a-standin' out here after just ridin' into town. Slip over to the Pine Tree with Vivie and she'll buy you a drink."

Her arm was in his.

"I'm not a pauper," Jim said.

She cocked her head and looked up at him saucily. She was, in a rough way, rather appealing—but the marks of her days were on her face and in her eyes and in her body.

"Texas man?"

Jim said, "Fish for information and you'll get none."

"Come on, Tex, an' drink with Vivie."

They crossed the street to the Pine Tree. Vivie shivered a little and let her teeth chatter.

"I should have pulled out and gone to New Orleans like I planned."

Jim asked, "Too late yet?"

She laughed and her laugh was deep in her throat. "Look, honey, look! It's this way, understand—a girl don't last long in this racket and she goes down and down and down, savvy?"

Jim said nothing.

"Finally she lands in a dump like this."

"It ain't much of a town," Jim conceded.

"A good spot to hide out in," she said.

Jim could almost feel her eyes on his face. He grinned. "Still fishin', eh? Try a different bait?"

She said, "Damn you, Tex, I like you."

They were inside the saloon. Vivie shivered and ran over to the pot-bellied wood stove and held her hands in front of it.

"Your blood's gettin' cold."

The words came from the bartender. He was a beefy man, built like a bull, and he had no neck—his head looked like it was set directly on his shoulders. Pale blue eyes laid against Jim in a seemingly disinterested manner.

"What will it be, stranger?"

Vivie said, "Tex is his name. I'd say he was from Texas seein' he talks like he does."

Three men were playing cards at the far table. One glanced up in open curiosity but the other two were more schooled and, although they seemed busy consulting their cards, Jim knew he was still under a minute scrutiny.

Tobacco smoke was thick in the place. A sawdust floor, a pot-bellied stove, and a small floor at the far end, evidently for dancing. Somewhere Jim heard the faint brassy tinkle of a piano.

It came from upstairs. He heard a woman laugh, and that came from upstairs, too. He ordered whiskey and he noticed Vivie drank a full shot, not something poured under the bar.

She said, "You wanna go upstairs with Vivie?"

Jim shook his head.

"You're turnin' me down?"

"It looks that way."

She didn't get angry, although she pouted a little. She hung onto his arm even closer.

"You know, I *do* like you, Tex."

"Forget the Tex. That ain't my name."

"Tex is a good name."

He put his back to the bar and hooked his elbows over the top rail and looked at the joint. That shot of whiskey that lay in his belly was liquid fire. He lit a match and held it in front of his mouth as he blew air.

"What the hell you tryin' to do?" the barkeeper asked.

"Seein' if the vapor will explode."

The beefy man made with what was supposed to be a smile. "I got some even stronger."

"Give it to Vivie."

Vivie began, "Tex, you come with me." She started pulling on his arm. She was a little too drunk, Jim realized. He pushed her and he did not push hard but she slipped and fell down in the sawdust.

Her dress came up and showed her thighs and she sat and cursed him.

A wide man pushed back his chair and came over to Jim, swaggering as he walked. He had a wide, hard-looking face, marked by a deep scar on his jaw.

"Mister," he said, "you're new here, but we don't push women around here, you understan'?"

"An accident," Jim murmured.

Vivie said, "Git to your seat, Rolf Palmer, an' let us alone! I ain't askin' you to put in your big oar!"

But Palmer had only eyes for Jim. "Jes' remember thet," he warned.

Jim said, "An' remember this, fella!" His left went straight out and smacked Rolf Palmer full on the mouth. Palmer flailed his arms and went back against the far wall, tipping over the card table. Cards and chips went in every direction. Palmer's eyes were filled with raw hell and he wiped his mouth. He took his hand down and looked at the blood on his palm.

"Fella, you hit the wrong man!"

Vivie screamed, "Tex, he's killed men with his hands! Tex, watch out—"

Palmer rushed ahead. Jim grabbed a chair. It made a sharp arc. The back of the heavy seat smacked Palmer on the head.

Rolf Palmer didn't even have time to grunt. He tried to duck but he was too slow. He crashed into the bar; it was solid and had no give. He spread out his arms and slid to a sitting-down position with his back to the bar.

His mouth came open and he had a foolish look.

The bartender came around the corner. He said, "Out cold, just like that. First time I've ever seen Palmer knocked out."

Jim said, "No use me wastin' knuckles on his hard head."

"A fight is a fight," the bartender said. "The main thing is to win it. If you're smart you'll hightail outa town, though. Palmer'll come to an' he'll drag for his iron, mister."

"I tote an iron too," Jim reminded.

Vivie got to her feet. "He had no right

to jump Tex that-a-way. Tex never knocked me down. I jest slipped."

The bartender had two men carry Rolf Palmer into a back room. Jim glanced up the back stairs and caught sight of two feminine faces peering down. The girls who owned the faces had very little clothing on. Jim put his eyes back on the rest of the saloon's occupants. So far he had not seen Rusty. Nor had he seen anybody with red hair, either.

Maybe he was riding a wild hunch?

"Another drink?" Vivie asked.

Jim shook his head. "I ain't halter-broke the last one yet," he said, smiling. Behind him Beefy wiped the bar with a damp towel. "Who's the boss of this burg, Beefy?"

"When The Boss wants you he'll send for you."

Jim grinned. "Hope it's danged sudden. I need some jack. The ol' larder is kinda small."

"If The Boss wants you you'll get credit aroun' town."

"I hope he wants me," Jim said.

He started for the door and Vivie said, "I'll go with you, Tex, an' show you where to find the beanery."

"I'm ol' enough to go aroun' alone."

Vivie pouted, red lips pursed. "You always hurt me, Tex. Why are you so mean to me?"

Jim went outside. Behind him trooped an old recluse who had been seated against the far wall.

"For a dime, mister," he whined, "I'll give you some information about Vivie."

Jim thought he'd humor him, so he gave him a quarter. "Rolf Palmer claims Vivie is his woman."

Jim said, "It wasn't worth a quarter," and went across the street toward a building that sported a sign, Wong Low's Chuck House. So far he had seen no sign of Rusty, had heard nothing that would give him a clue as to Rusty's whereabouts, if the red-headed rider had been Rusty. The barn had not harbored a buckskin, either. Maybe his eyes were bad, at that.

But he knew this would be a slow—and dangerous—game.

This town of Larb City was a rough one, no two ways about that. It would be just the environment that Rusty would like, at that. Tough men, easy money, and easy women. Rusty would like it here.

Inside Wong Low's it was warm and he caught the good smell of roast beef. He was the cafe's only occupant. He spun a stool and sat down and soon Wong Low waddled out of the kitchen. Jim ordered roast beef and all the trimmings. Wong Low served him and then stood opposite him.

"You new boy here?"

"Just rode in," Jim said.

"Somebody rob county clerk down in Beaver Tail, eh?"

"Haven't heard a word about it, Wong."

Jim wasn't sure, but he thought Wong Low smiled a little.

"You catch'm pardner?"

Jim looked up. "Me have a pardner? Why, I've never thought of such a thing. Why ask?"

"Toast burn," Wong grunted, and Jim watched his broad back wobble back into the kitchen.

Jim finished his meal without interference. Back in the kitchen Wong Low shuffled around and made noises with his pots. Jim found himself missing Bootjack. For years he and the big man had ridden together and to lose Bootjack would be like losing his right arm. But he realized he and his friend were playing a dangerous game. And for a while they would both have to ride separate trails.

Vivie had been sicced on him to try to get information out of him. He was sure of that. He had made a deadly enemy in Rolf Palmer. But he had shown right off that he was tough, and the denizens of Larb City would not forget the quick and efficient manner he had used to put Palmer out of circulation.

His meal finished, he called, "How much are the damages, Wong?"

"One buck."

"Cheap at half the price."

Jim laid a silver dollar on the clean

counter. Picking his teeth, his inner man satisfied, he went toward the livery-barn. He glanced suddenly toward a log building. A curtain moved a little. His every move was being watched.

Eyes. Eyes everywhere.

"Leavin' so soon?" the hostler said. "Palmer runnin' you outa town?"

Jim spat into the manure. "That for Palmer. Nope, I aim to stay here a few days. Lookin' for work."

"You might find work here."

"Might not be the right kind."

"*Might* be, too."

Jim glanced at his saddle. He saw immediately that his saddlebags and bedroll had been disturbed. Somebody had gone through his belongings. He was lucky he had cached Janet's badge.

Had they found the badge in his belongings it would have been too bad for him.

He remembered Janet's clean, girlish face; he compared it with Vivie's hard-shelled look.

Jim said, "Who went through my saddlebags an' unrolled my bed?"

The hostler showed a blank, almost hurt, look. "Why, mister, nobody done went through your stuff."

Jim only smiled.

"Where about's in this burg can a man get a bunk?"

"They's rooms for rent above the saloon."

Jim shook his head. "I just want a room," he reminded. "Not a woman with it."

The hostler studied him as though he were a queer animal. Jim knew his answer was not logical but the hostler did not know he was thinking about Janet Albers.

"Reckon mebbe you can bunk up in the haymow, that is if you don't smoke. An' that's on condition thet the Big Boss says I can let you sleep there."

"The Big Boss sure runs this burg."

Jim received no answer to this. Later the hostler met him down town and said,

"Okay for the haymow, if you don't smoke."

Jim nodded.

8

JIM lay in the quiet of the livery-barn haymow and smoked a cigaret, the coal glowing and ebbing as he sucked. A hot ash fell into the hay and he watched it make a fiery ring. When the ring got about an inch wide he jabbed his thumb down on it and killed it.

Below him horses chewed, their jaws making sounds. The hay was wild blue-joint and the smell of it was sweet and good. But Jim wasn't interested in the hay nor was he interested in the horses. He was interested in a red-headed man and a buckskin horse called Sonny.

His cigaret dead, he laced his hands behind his head, and gazed up at the roof of the barn, and he had his thoughts. So far he had accomplished nothing. He wondered what Bootjack was doing, back at the homestead. If Rusty wanted to look him up Rusty would go to the site of the new homestead and he would meet Bootjack. That is, if the red-head had been Rusty.

Anyway, Rusty did not seem to be in Larb City. If Rusty was in town, then Jim had not seen him; neither had he seen the Sonny horse, either.

Gradually the town became quiet. At last even the shouts and noise from the Pine Tree became things of the past. Jim slipped on his boots and climbed down the ladder and stood on the ground floor. A horse smelled him and snorted softly.

"Steady, boy."

Evidently the hostler was asleep in his small office. Jim went quietly past his domicile and was outside. His plan was to look around and see if he could locate Sonny in some other barn in Larb City. Once he found the horse he would stay close to him and eventually Rusty would come for his mount.

He stiffened, hidden in shadows.

Larb City lay under the pale northern moonlight. Ugly and profane and sin-laden, it looked almost pretty under the moon. Jim thought he had seen a man move ahead of him, but he was not sure. The moonlight made for many shadows —shifting, mirage—dim shadows.

He knew he was under constant surveillance.

He waited, silent, watching. He judged he waited about half an hour. The night was none too warm at this high altitude although the wind had died. Finally, he moved down an alley. A tin can reflected moonbeams and lay glistening like a white jewel in the dust. He came to a log building and the smell of manure told him it was a barn.

Horses chewed on hay. The place held the close heavy odor of horseflesh. But the barn was very dark—so dark he could not determine the number of horses inside, or their colors.

He thumbed a match into quick life, then extinguished it.

Two bays, a black and a sorrel—but not a buckskin. Sonny was not in this barn, and the barn was behind the Pine Tree Saloon, too. Jim slid outside. Then, for the second time, he stiffened, tense and tough in the shadows.

A man had moved back into the shadows, up there ahead of him about fifty feet. He was sure it was a man, although he had only caught a glimpse of a movement back into the darkness. He went back into the barn. His exploring fingers found a chunk of two by four railing loose along the top of the manger. He juggled this, and smiled. Then he scrambled out the hay-window. The window was none too big but he wriggled through it, club and all, to stand on the ground behind the small barn.

He juggled the club for feel.

Satisfied, he went on tip-toe along the south wall of the barn, and he flattened himself there, the logs rough against his back. Across town a dog talked to a coyote back in the foothills. High on the ridges the wind moved through the pines and the sound was like that of flowing water.

Jim waited.

Finally, after what seemed eternity, a

man moved along the side of a building trying to keep the shadows around him. He worked his way toward the barn. He had to cross a moonlit strip and Jim recognized him as Rolf Palmer.

Palmer had been ordered to trail him.

Or was Palmer out for revenge?

Jim grinned.

The club rose and came down. Rolf Palmer grunted, "Ugh," and for the second time that day Jim knocked him cold. But Palmer carried his six-shooter in his hand. Reflex action and training were so strong they made him let the hammer drop.

The lead sang into space. The roar was loud in the night. Jim was moving fast. He cut across a vacant lot and came to the rear door of the barn. Up front the old hostler was stirring and he had lit his lamp.

Out in the alley a man hollered, "Palmer's done out like a blowed-out lamp, men! Layin' here in the alley—"

"Who did the shootin'?" another man demanded.

The hostler ran out, carrying a rifle. Jim climbed the rickety ladder and hit his sougans. Gradually the town quieted again. He heard somebody climbing the ladder and he lay in the dark with his six-shooter under his blankets.

"It's me, the hostler."

Jim feigned slumber.

"I say it's me, fella. Ike, the hostler."

"What the hell you want, man? Get outa here an' let a payin' customer sleep!"

"You must be a sound sleeper. Didn't the commotion wake you up?"

"What commotion?"

"Somebody had slugged Rolf Palmer. Smacked him over the head with a two by four. They'd found Palmer in front of the Pine Tree Saloon's stable."

"Well, what about it?" Jim asked.

"Nobody knows who did it. Not even Palmer. He came to in the doc's office an' he didn't even know what had happened to him."

"He ain't git no brains."

Jim rolled over.

The hostler chewed tobacco and spat.

Jim knew the man had come to check on his presence.

Jim said, "Well, you've checked on me, now get out of here."

"Well, now, don't get testy—"

Jim was on his back. He raised both legs, cocked his feet, and let the hostler get both in his chest. The man went down and sat in the hay.

"Get out," Jim ordered.

"You oughta not kick a man like thet—"

"Make tracks or I'll—"

There was no need to finish the sentence. The man was already hastily scrambling down the ladder. Jim grinned in the dark. He had to show the Big Boss he was a tough one, for maybe the Big Boss—whoever he was—would lead him to Rusty. The hostler would bellyache to the Big Boss.

Jim didn't sleep the rest of the night, though.

But when he came into Wong Low's at about ten in the morning he was yawning as though he'd had a good night's rest.

Already he had shaved himself, using the watering trough as a source of water.

"Heard they had a little commotion last night," he said.

Wong Low's wide face had no expression. "Me no hear about commotion. You want breakfast?"

His meal finished, Jim loafed around town. He had been in tough towns before but this seemed to be the toughest of the tough. He dare not make a question that pointed toward the red-head who held up the clerk's office. If he did so these hard-cases would jump to the immediate conclusion he was a lawman, and he had a hunch lawmen didn't live long in this town.

Therefore he was surprised when Sheriff Mike Albers rode boldly into town that same afternoon.

Jim was in the Pine Tree Saloon and Vivie was standing close to him at the bar. Rolf Palmer was playing cards with three men at a far table and now and then Jim caught the big man eyeing him truculently. Palmer had a big bruise on the back of his neck and Jim figured sure that the man also sported a slight headache.

Jim said, "Who's that hairpin, Vivie?"

Vivie told him that the rider was Sheriff Mike Albers and Jim pretended he did not know the lawman. Albers dismounted in front of the saloon and came inside, and to Jim's surprise he apparently did not recognize him. Jim was sure, also, that the sheriff should know him, what with their little tussle back in the canyon when Bootjack's Justin had knocked Albers into sleep.

Beefy leaned both hairy hands on the bar. "What'll it be, sheriff?"

"Beer, Beefy, and two bandits. The ones that held up the clerk's office."

"I can deliver the beer," Beefy said, "but I can't deliver the bandits." He slid out a cold bottle of beer. "Havin' any luck, sheriff?"

"Not a bit, Beefy."

The whole saloon was listening. Jim expected the lawman to pull a gun on him any moment. But instead of drawing on him Sheriff Albers said, "Have a beer with me, fella?"

"Don't mind if I do, and thanks."

"One for the lady, too," Albers said.

Vivie said, "Thanks, sheriff, but make mine bourbon, Beefy."

Albers shrugged thin shoulders and glanced at Jim. "She likes 'em strong, eh? Bottoms toward the ceiling."

They drank. Albers said so-long and went outside. An hour later he rode out of town, heading east.

"Goin' over to Ledo town," Beefy said. "That's the end of his county, too. Guess them bandits got plumb away."

"Odd he didn't jump me," Jim said slowly. "His daughter accused me of helpin' them two—claimed we was stooges down in town for 'em." He laughed.

"Maybe he's changed his mind," Beefy allowed.

"Maybe you were in with them!"

The words were harsh and domineering and they came from Rolf Palmer. Jim turned and looked at the man and read the raw hate in the big whiskery face. He knew then that if he stayed around town he'd have to kill Palmer, or Rolf Palmer would kill him.

"Maybe I was," Jim agreed.

Palmer was surprised by this answer and his face showed this. He muttered something Jim could not hear, glared at Vivie who spat at him, and then back to study his cards.

"Maybe you've held up a bank or two?"

Jim's voice was quiet as he addressed the gunman.

Palmer looked up. "What the hell's it to you?"

Jim almost called the man, and then discretion came in and checked his tongue. But his gaze was level as he said, "Mister, don't rub me, savvy?"

Jim bought another two drinks. "The bankroll is gettin' slim."

Beefy nodded.

Vivie said, "Don't worry, Tex."

"I'm not." Jim smiled.

He had deliberately stressed the fact he

was almost broke. He wanted to get on the inside track and maybe then, if he could get the Big Boss' confidence, he could find out something about the redhead. Maybe the Big Boss would send him on a raid. But even at that, the statement was true. He was getting flat in the pocket-book.

Actually, he should have had money, and he would have had dinero—had not the U U trailherd so mysteriously disappeared. But that was water under the bridge, that was gunpowder already fired; still, the loss of the herd had hit him hard financially.

What had happened to the herd?

Had it been rustled and sold in some eastern stockyard—Chicago, for instance—after being driven to a railroad in the Dakotas? He had checked via the mails with the eastern slaughterhouses but had found no record of U U cattle being shipped in for slaughter. But of course he had not covered all stockyards. There were bound to be some to which he had not written.

He was sure the herd had been rustled. Mining towns were sprouting up in this area—in the Black Hills to the east gold had been discovered and towns had come out of the earth—and these towns needed beef. And most of the unscrupulous mine owners, with a gang of miners to feed, didn't care where their beef came from or what brand it packed—just so they got it cheap enough.

Then, too, there was this conciliatory manner of Sheriff Mike Albers. By all rights, the sheriff should have tried to arrest him.

Jim didn't understand it.

But he did know one thing: the fact that he had had a drink with the sheriff had public opinion against him. Had he used his full presence of mind he would have turned down the lawman's offer harshly. But the offer had come so unexpectedly, so sudden, he had not considered its full significance. And he had drunk with the lawman and thereby turned the suspicion of these longriders against him.

"I gotta git some work," he told Beefy. "Or else go on your cuff."

"If the Big Boss says you can go on credit."

"I'd like to work with the Big Boss, whoever he is."

"Stick around, son."

"Not with no dinero an' when there're safes an' railroad trains runnin'."

Beefy said nothing.

Rolf Palmer nursed his grouch and watched under thick eyebrows. Vivie hung onto Jim as though she aimed to marry him. She wanted him to leave the haymow and share her room. Jim thought of Janet Albers again, and said maybe he would, later on. To this Vivie's eyebrows went up. She couldn't understand this.

"If I offered Rolf the chance to share my bunk he'd jump at it," she pouted. "Are you a well man?"

"Doc done tol' me I'd live to ninety."

"You will, too . . . unless Rolf gets you."

"He's jealous of you."

Vivie said, "Honey, I can't stay away

from you." She put her arm around his neck and kissed him; she was rather well oiled.

Rolf Palmer saw the kiss and he scowled.

He jumped Jim that afternoon. Jumped him on the main street. They went for their guns. Palmer was fast, fast as the wind; Jim got him, though. The shot was hurriedly placed and it broke Palmer's left shoulder. He went down in the dust and Jim got his gun.

Beefy said, "My Gawd, you can sure handle that cutter!"

"I've had practice."

Vivie said, "Honey, are you hurt?"

Jim shook his head. "His lead took to the dust." He was a little sick of it all. For a moment he thought, *to hell with Rusty*, and then he knew he could never live the rest of his life with the riddle of his brother's disappearance unsolved.

Palmer sat there, holding his shoulder, and he glared silently at Jim. The doc—an old bloated drunk—worked on him. Jim met Palmer's eyes and read even a greater hate there. Actually he had shot to kill; under the great pressure, though, he had missed the man's heart.

Palmer said, "I'll kill you yet."

Jim merely nodded.

Back in the Pine Tree Saloon Jim and Vivie drank. Beefy said, "He's out to get you, Tex."

"I should have killed him," Jim admitted.

A little bell jangled upstairs. A flunky climbed the stairs and when he came down he sidled close to Jim.

"Big Boss wants to see you," he said.

Jim hid his surprise.

Beefy said, "Follow me."

Jim followed the wide man up the stairs. They came to a long hall that ran the length of the Pine Tree. A side door opened and a harpy looked out. She didn't have on too much clothing.

Beefy said, "No customer, girl. The Big Boss wants to see him."

Bold eyes studied Jim. "I don't want him nohow. I don't want that Vivie cutting my throat."

9

BEEFY opened a door. "This is the room."

Jim went into a room that was absolutely empty except for a bench along the far side. A small room it was, and there was an opening high in the wall. It had a grill across it and it was about two feet square.

A voice said, "That's all, Beefy. Go back to your bar work."

The voice was very strange. It almost boomed into the small room. Jim realized it had come through the grill and it sounded as though the Big Boss spoke through a long tube to disguise his voice.

Beefy said "Okay, Boss," and left.

Jim stood in the room, a little perplexed. This was eerie. You stood in a bare room, facing a bare wall, and a voice came out of a grill. Then, too, you were aware of eyes watching you—eyes that probed you—and you didn't know where they were. Then finally he gave up looking.

"Sit down, Jim Carlin."

Again, that long-drawn, echoing voice.

Jim sat on the bench. The Big Boss had called him *Jim Carlin* and that told him he could hide nothing from the man, whoever he was. For evidently the Big Boss had spies all over. He had got Jim's true name off the files of the clerk in the land office, Jim figured.

Jim asked, "What do you want?" and his words were loud in the small room, although he spoke in a normal tone of voice.

"It isn't what I want, mister, it's what you want that we'll talk about. You're after somebody here, or something. What is it?"

"You're so smart," Jim said, "you tell me!"

"You've hinted that you wanted a *job*." Jim listened carefully but he could not recognize the voice and finally he gave up. The voice evidently came from another room through a tube. But how did the Big Boss watch him? Jim glanced straight up. For the first time he noticed the lens set in the ceiling. He judged that this was part of a periscopic machine that allowed the Big Boss to see him, but he could not see the Big Boss.

Now that his nerves had lost some of their tension, the deadliness of this set-up fascinated him.

"What are you after here?"

Jim said, "That's my business."

There was a long moment of silence—and Jim felt his nerves knot again. Then a low chuckle came over the tube and the Big Boss said, "Mister, I don't trust you, savvy? But stick around town for a spell. There might be a job for you later on . . . and there might not be."

Jim got to his feet. "Is that all?"

"That's all."

Jim started for the door but the Big Boss' voice stopped him.

"You fool nobody," the voice boomed. "Only yourself."

"What do you mean by that?"

"You make a guess."

Jim said, "I don't understand."

"Get out of the room," the voice said.

Jim went outside into the hall. He was almost shivering despite his efforts to remain calm. The eeriness, the uncanny cleverness of the Big Boss, struck him with full significance; the realization became even stronger that he was in danger. He had learned nothing except that he was being watched. The Big Boss had hinted at much but had said darned little.

Above all these thoughts was the one that told him he was in danger of being killed. He was sure, now, he was on the right track. But the Big Boss knew that Jim Carlin and Rusty Carlin were related. Jim wished now he had not filed on that homestead; if he had come under a fictitious name his chances of finding the lost U U trainherd—and Rusty and Pancho Torres—would have been greater. But he had fallen in love with the Hell Creek region and he and Bootjack had decided it would make a good place to settle on and use for headquarters in their hunt. But they had made an error, the way things had turned out.

Well, he couldn't repeal the past.

He felt sure that Rusty was not in Larb City. He had not seen a red-head in the few days he had loafed around this little burg. He decided he would leave the town when night came.

If he were still alive when the sun sank.

He went down the steps, thinking this over; Vivie hooked arms with him. Jim realized the girl had gone all-out for him and he did not like this thought. She was cute in a crude, worn way; she was not for him. It seemed odd that she who had known so many men would fall in love with him. Maybe it was because he had not made a play for her and he had turned her down? Whatever it was, it was of no moment; his objective was to get out of Larb City.

The Big Boss knew his real name, and if the Big Boss had been in on stealing the U U trailherd . . .

"Did you join up, honey?"

"Up to the Big Boss," Jim said.

"He'll let you tie into the bunch. He hates Rolf Palmer and you sure trimmed his sails."

Jim nodded.

There was another angle to consider, too. Sheriff Mike Albers had not arrested him; that did not make sense. Maybe the lawman had talked with Bootjack and Bootjack had talked him into dropping charges against them? There was a little logic in that, Jim reasoned. And Albers had not dared mention this fact before Beefy and the hard-cases in the Pine Tree Saloon.

Jim walked to the edge of Larb City. A man came across the trail and he carried a .30-.30 rifle. He was on foot.

"Huntin' rabbits," the man explained.

Jim nodded.

The man went through the sagebrush toward a high hill that overlooked the trail and a jackrabbit jumped up ahead of him. The rabbit went a few rods and then sat up on his hindlegs, making an easy shot. Still, the man did not shoot.

Jim thought, hunting rabbits with a Winchester .30-.30 that would blow a pack to pieces. And then he doesn't even shoot when he sees one . . .

Hunting rabbits, baloney.

He went back to the mainstreet and walked toward the road that led to Ledo. Here was another hunter, also equipped with a .30-.30 rifle. There was no *hunter* barring the trail that ran down toward Beaver Tail town. But Jim caught the flash of sunlight on steel high in the rocks. That flash had been deliberate, he knew. It was a warning that he was being watched.

There was ice along Jim Carlin's spine. The heavy weight of his gun felt strong on his thigh. His gun was his only friend.

He went back to the saloon. Beefy seemed cold and unfriendly; men regarded him with short stares and short nods. Only Vivie seemed as cordial as ever. Still, her laugh seemed a little too high, her color too strong even though her rouge was heavy. Once he caught her looking at him rather pensively.

"I'm not dead yet, woman."

"I don't—understand."

He spoke softly. "Why don't you stay away from me, girl? They've got me marked and they aim to kill me."

"Because of Palmer?"

He shook his head. "Somethin' bigger, honey."

But still she stayed close to him.

He did not take a drink the rest of the day. He built his plan of action—he would not ride out on his horse, for the bronc would be watched, too. He would steal a horse from a hitchrack or out of the barn behind the Pine Tree. Darkness came, the big kerosene lamps were lit and spread their sticky stink, and voices rose and tobacco smoke became a cloud. Palmer had sworn to kill him and by tomorrow Palmer would be walking around. Vivie disclosed this to him.

"Me for the hay," Jim said, and yawned.

He left Vivie in the saloon and he went to the barn. He lay back in the hay and smoked and thought. Gradually the town quieted, and finally the Pine Tree darkened; Jim glanced at his watch in the moonlight and by peering could see the hour hand was close to three.

He did not go down the ladder. He dropped out the haymow door, fell about ten feet to the ground, landing like a cat. A few minutes later he was in the barn behind the Pine Tree. He saddled a horse and led him out. He was on his way, and fierce exultation pounded in his blood.

Then something hard hit him a ringing blow on the back of his head. He went down, lurching ahead; he had not heard the boots behind him.

A voice growled, "Get him and kill him!"

They were on him, then; they were dark shapes, with clubs, with guns. He didn't have a chance. The unexpected blow had stunned him; his gun was gone. He fought as best he could, but he knew his efforts were almost futile.

He smashed a man in the mouth. The man went down and his gun skidded. Jim got the weapon, the feel of it cold against his palm, and he shot a man through the chest, and the man went down.

"He's got Rube's gun!"

"Slug him down!"

A hard, slim object hit him in the neck. Somebody had slugged him with a rifle's barrel. This time Jim went to his knees.

"Over there," a man hollered. "In them shadows by the saloon. He's got a partner! I seen a man with a gun!"

Gun flame came from the saloon. A man grunted, went down. Jim sat there, stunned, powerless to move. His first thought was that Bootjack had come to help him. Or maybe Rusty was alive—maybe Rusty had come to help his brother—

Guns talked. The man came out of the shadows, stumbling out, and he saw through a thickening blur that it was not a man, it was Vivie.

She gasped. "Don't shoot me!"

"The girl!"

"Vivie!"

Jim tried to rise, got to his hands and knees, and a boot kicked his hands out from under him, making him land on his face. He rolled over and Vivie fell beside him, her dress ballooning out.

"Tex, they shot me, Tex! I wanted to help you—"

There was more than anger in Jim Carlin. There was a rage, a blind, wild rage, the rage that makes a man ten times more powerful as he is in moments of sanity. This immoral girl, this tramp, had tried to save him; they had shot her. He got to his feet.

He did not know he finally hit the ground on his face. For he was unconscious when he fell.

An outlaw had slugged him with a two by four.

It was the same two by four he had used to knock out Rolf Palmer!

10

FIRST he felt pain. Pain in his head. Gradually this settled down and he became aware of things. There was the dark. There was the rough clods under him. He got an elbow under his side and raised himself.

Giddiness enveloped him; he bent his head; he waited. Finally it fell back, also; he looked around him.

Only blackness. Inky blackness.

He heard somebody breathing. A hoarse, deep, guttural breathing.

"Who's that?"

"Vivie, Tex."

He remembered, then.

"They knocked me out?"

"Yes, and they threw us in here."

"They shot you," he reminded.

"Through the chest, Tex. I had to help you."

He crept to her. He got the impression

they were in a small house; the air was close, almost weighty. He felt of the wall. The rough feel of sod met his fingers. He found her in the dark. She was soft and warm; she put her arms around him—Jim found her lips. They were alone and they were sick and they were outcasts; all this was in their embrace.

"How are you? Did they bandage you?"

"No, they just threw me in here, with you. How are you, Tex?"

"My real name is Jim," he corrected. "Jim Carlin."

"Oh."

Her arms relaxed.

"Carlin," she said. "That sounds—familiar."

Jim's heart jumped. "Rusty?"

She was silent, only her breathing was heard.

"I—I don't know, Jim. Jim, am I going to die here? Tell me I'm not, Jim, please."

She was a child, girlish and small; she wanted assurance. Jim felt as though there was no justice in the world. None at all.

"Honey," he said, "trust me, please." And he kissed her again.

"Jim, I haven't been a good girl."

"Hush."

His hands made explorations. The bullet had ripped through the outer edge of her right breast. It had gone through; her side was a sticky mess. Jim took his shirt and wiped blood away carefully in the dark.

"Am I hurt bad, Jim? My ribs must be broken, it's so hard to breathe. Did the bullet go through?"

"The bullet tore its way out."

"That's good. I feel better already. I've stopped bleeding. That's a good sign. Isn't that a good sign, Jim?"

Jim assured her it was. "Where are we?"

She told him they were in a cabin behind the store. Jim expressed his desire to know what they intended to do with them now that the Big Boss' men had them prisoners.

"Wonder why they didn't kill me?" he asked.

"The Big Boss is out of town, I understand. They don't dare kill you until he comes back an' gives orders."

"Who is he?"

"I don't know. I doubt if anybody knows. Yes, somebody must know. I think they went out to hold up a train."

Jim considered this. Why did not Sheriff Mike Albers get a posse and clean out this outlaw hangout? He voiced this fact to Vivie who said that Albers, it seemed, could never get any direct evidence against any of Larb City's denizens. All he had, Vivie figured, were strong suspicions.

"Or else he's bein' paid," Jim ventured.

They were silent, there in the darkness. Outside a man paced back and forth, occasionally stopping to rest; a guard, Jim Carlin knew. Vivie's breathing had lost its terrible harshness and had settled down to a steady wheezing sound. Jim did not like that sound one bit and his heart went out to the girl who had tried to save him. Fate spun an odd loop and a man never knew just whom the noose would encircle next.

"You ever see a red-headed guy around Larb City?"

He spoke quietly so the guard could not hear.

"No, I haven't."

"One held up the county clerk's office. I saw him right close. He had a mask on so I couldn't see his face."

"I've heard about that red-head, but I've never seen him."

"You ever see a Mex around here?" He described Pancho Torres. "An ol' man, he is. His name is Pancho."

"I've—I've heard of him, Jim."

"What do you mean by that?"

"I've heard them talk in the saloon about him. Some call him the Wild Man. He's out in the badlands—they say his head is twisted—his brain is crazy—Jim, I'm tired."

"Sleep, honey."

"Jim, hold Vivie."

Finally she slept, despite her pain. She was small and fragile, and Jim wondered about the frail body—would it hold up under its wound? He had to get out of here. When the Big Boss came back the Big Boss would order him shot.

And Jim Carlin didn't want to be shot. He wanted to find out what had become of Rusty Carlin and old Pancho Torres and a big herd of U U cows. And he wanted to settle down on Hell Creek and build a long, rambling log house. He wanted to have a wheat field and a patch of good spuds.

But how would he get out?

He explored the room, feeling the walls. Not a window in the place, not a stick of furniture, not even a lamp. Just a dirt floor and a sod roof and sod walls. He went back and felt along the ground and found Vivie, who was still sleeping. He got the wild, uncontrollable feeling that he was doomed, that he was a hog being transported to the butcher's knife.

"Guard."

The pacing stopped.

"Oh, guard."

"What the hell you want?"

"This girl. Vivie. She's dyin'."

"Let her die."

Pacing again.

"Guard?"

"Spit it out, Carlin."

"Help her, for Gawd's sake. Be a human, not a beast. Get the doc, an' hurry."

Silence.

"You hear me?"

"I heard you."

"Get the medico, please."

He heard the guard say, "Shorty, I'm steppin' inside, an' you take over the watch."

"Okay, Joe."

Jim watched the door open slowly. It swung outward on silent leather hinges. Lantern light showed and then a man moved into the doorway. He had a .45 in his hand and the light made reflections on the gun's barrel. Jim could not see his face too clearly, for the lantern had a dim light; nevertheless he had a heavy, bearded face—he recognized it as belonging to a thug he had seen a number of times in the Pine Tree Saloon.

"Jus' stand where you are, Carlin!"

Jim said, "I'll do nothin'. Just help the girl."

The man looked at Vivie. Jim's plan was that perhaps the man would get to his knees to inspect the girl and then Jim would jump him. It was a wild plan, born of wild desire and demand, and Jim was wild with anxiety. But he never got a chance. The man went to his knees, yes; he ran rough hands over Vivie, and his back was toward Jim; still, Jim could not jump him. For the second guard had moved into the doorway and he also carried a lantern that he set just inside the door. And he spread his thin legs wide and drew his other short-gun. He had two guns and he stood there and he watched Jim like a cat watches a gopher-hole.

Jim thought, *I haven't got a chance. They'd kill me like a boot stomps out an ant.*

"Jes' take it plumb easy," the man in the doorway advised.

Jim said, "I'm no damn' fool, fella."

"I got my doubts about that."

The first man took another feel of Vivie. Evidently he found an animal-pleasure in fondling the girl's body. Vivie did not open her eyes. Finally the man stood up and spoke to the guard in the door.

"Hell, she'll pull through, Shorty."

Shorty said, "A deal to get you inside to try to dump you." He swung his right hand gun and fired point-blank at Jim.

Jim jumped to his right. The roar was very loud in the small room. He thought at first that the man aimed to kill him and then, when he realized the bullet had missed, he got the impression that the man had fired only to scare him and not to hit him.

Vivie sat up. "Jim, lover, are you all right?"

Shorty grinned, lantern-light making his eyes evil-looking jewels that sparkled. "Only shot to scare him, *lover*."

Joe said, "Cover me while I go outside, Shorty?" and Shorty nodded. Joe pushed past his partner and went outside. Shorty moved out of the doorway and the door went shut and Jim heard the bolt outside click. Then he heard a brace slide into a bracket; the door was also barred with a brace across it.

"It didn't work," he said.

He squatted beside Vivie.

"I feel stronger."

Jim said, "I don't know how the hell we'll get out of here."

"Just have trust and faith, Jim."

They were strange words coming from the painted lips of a dancehall girl, but to Jim they were comforting words. He also found comfort in the thought that he might have outside help in the person of Bootjack James. If Bootjack had some way of being informed that Jim was in danger—

His hand held Vivie's. He discovered that he was thinking of Janet Albers. What would she do if she had been forced into a predicament like the one Vivie was in? Would she bear up with the same courage, the same fortitude, that Vivie was showing?

Jim thought, *She would. I know she would.*

Morning came and light seeped under the door. The day passed and night came again and they had not received water or chuck nor had the bloated drunken doc come to see Vivie.

Vivie improved a little, Jim thought, in the forenoon. Then later on in the day she became very sick. Fever was hot in her, putting fire into her body; she clung to his hand and begged for water. Jim appealed to the guards and got only rebuffs. They would not even open the door. None would enter.

"She needs water, men. Are you human?"

"Shut your mouth, man!"

Jim wished now he had jumped Joe, even though the odds would have been terribly large against him. Then common sense told him Shorty would have shot him to ribbons had he made a move toward Joe. But if another guard entered the sod room, Jim would jump him—even if there was a cannon pointing at him.

He walked the room, measuring his strides. Four the length of the room, two the width. He was so hungry his belly must have thought his throat was cut. He was so dry his mouth was cotton.

Why didn't the Big Boss—whoever the gent was—come in and give an order to take them out of this stinking room?

Darkness came and the dim light showing under the door became a thing of the past. Jim sat beside Vivie who moaned and cried in her sleep. He tried to swallow and couldn't; Lord, were they even humans? No, they were devils.

Suddenly he came to his feet.

Outside he had heard a dull thud. He thought, Somebody got slugged, sure as heck, and wild hope speared through him. Had Bootjack—good old Bootjack—come into Larb City and had he found out where his pard was jailed? He heard something that sounded like a man's body hitting the ground. But the thickness of the walls made sound a hard element to judge.

A body brushed against the outside wall. Jim heard the latch lift, heard the bolt click open. He saw the door swing outward.

"Carlin?"

The voice did not belong to Bootjack. Then whose voice was it? Jim could not see the man clearly. He could only see the wide form of him.

"Yes, this is Carlin."

"Here's your .45 an' your gunbelt. Make tracks outa here pronto."

"Who are you?"

Jim got no answer, for the man seemed to melt into the night. He went to the open door and listened and peered but heard nothing. Then down at the Pine Tree a fiddle started squeaking and a piano made thin noises.

The guard lay beside the wall, a dark inert heap.

Jim wondered, *What the heck?*

Was this a trick to get him to walk out

and shoot him down, just for target practice? He wondered if his .45 had cartridges in its cylinder. The feel and heft of it told him it was his outfit.

He broke the loading-gate. He jacked out a cartridge. He hefted it and decided it was about the right weight. His fingers told him it had lead in it. He realized he was armed again; he also figured he'd best get on his way right smart.

He got Vivie across his shoulders.

Carrying her, gun up, he moved into the alley, half-expecting fire to break out at him, to smash bullets into him. But no bullets came and he finally reached the livery-stable.

The old hostler hobbled out of his office. His wrinkled old face was screwed up into a fierce squint as he tried to identify his visitors, for his lantern's light blinded him.

"The-the stranger—"

Jim's .45 came down. The lantern fell and the glass broke. Coal oil ran across the floor and flame came with it. Jim grabbed a saddled bronc and spurred him out the back door.

Vivie had her arms around his waist; she rode behind him. Jim spurred the bronc down an alley-way and into the night. Back of them the old livery-man raised a loud din.

"They rode out the back—"

A gun spoke from between two buildings. Jim swung his horse slightly and answered fire, his .45 talking. Back in the shadows a man screamed and Jim caught a glimpse of him. He was about the size of Toad Graham—big as Toad, as broad as the O Bar O Connected gunman.

He did not shoot again.

Back of them men hollered as they ran for broncs. Jim fed his borrowed mount the steel and the darkness rushed down from the hills and hid them. Behind him Vivie bounced and he realized this wild ride was doing her wound no good.

"How you takin' it, girl?"

"I'll-I'll get through, Jim."

Grit, pure grit. Admiration touched

Jim. She was plucky, this girl; she had a stiff backbone.

They rode about two miles, and then Jim swung the bronc to the west, riding up a brushy draw. Wild rosebushes dragged their thorny claws across them and their mount, and Jim did his best to protect the wounded girl. He needed water and she was dying for water, and springs are always at the head of a draw—instinct and logic was taking him toward water.

"Listen, lover."

Out on the trail men rode with wild hoofs, driving onward. The hoofs ran out and Jim said, "They rode straight on. This darkness is our ally."

"We had another ally back there—the man who turned us loose."

"Did you recognize his voice?"

Her answer came slowly. "This may sound crazy, lover, but it—it sounded to me like he was Rolf Palmer."

"You know, it did sound like Palmer, a little."

"It couldn't have been him."

Jim shook his head. "It sure couldn't have been," he agreed. "Now to get you to some water and then into Beaver Tail to see the doc."

"There's a warrant for you down there. I heard the talk in the saloon. Mike Albers had it in his pocket the day he talked to you, I heard."

"Wonder why he didn't serve it?"

"He's got a plan, he has. He's a wise one, that sheriff. Oh, find water, please, lover, please."

Her voice, feverish and deadly sick, was terrible to hear.

Jim silently prayed that he would be able to get her to a town in time.

11

JIM found water not at the head of that draw, but at the head of another that was across a pine-crested ridge. There he found a little spring that bubbled out of the rocks. He carried Vivie to this and put her on the grass. She was bleeding again; her dress was wet and dark on the side; and she was unconscious. The hard, pounding ride had done her little good.

He put her on the grass and wet his shirt and laid it across her forehead. He washed her face carefully and he wet her lips. He had pity for the unfortunate girl and he had a deadly hate toward the men who had shot her. This pushed back even the desire to find out what had become of his brother and his old Mexican friend and the big U U trailherd. It put everything out of his mind except the clarion call for revenge. She had become wounded because she had fought to help him; he, then, was indirectly responsible for her suffering.

"Jim, we had better go. We're not far enough yet from Larb City, and if they find us it will be my fault—without me you'd have been in town by now."

"Hush, Vivie, don't say that."

"Leave me, Jim, and ride. You can come back for me, lover."

Jim said, "We stick together, girl."

Dawn found them on the trail that led to Beaver City. Vivie rode behind him, and her head dropped; Jim had his free hand back, and he held her as best he could. Finally she almost slid from the horse. He dismounted and got her in front of him, and she was limp and sick and lonesome; he had his arm around her slender waist, and so he held her.

A dog barked.

Sheriff Mike Albers came out of his office, pulling up his suspenders. He wore a red night-shirt which he had tucked into his pants.

"You're under arrest, Carlin."

"I have to get her to the doc's first," Jim said.

Janet Albers was in with the few early risers who greeted Jim and Vivie. Jim said, "You goin' to visit me when I'm in your clink?"

"I'll change your bracelets," the girl said.

She wasn't joking, either. She was eyeing Vivie rather truculently. Jim thought, *Holy Smoke, she looks like she's jealous!* Then he blamed it all on too much imagination.

A man said, "I woke up doc. He'll be out of his sougans right after he gets another drink."

Jim dismounted and carried Vivie into the doctor's office. There he laid her on a couch.

"Jim, you should have left me out in the hills, lover. Now you're going to go to jail all on account of me—"

"Hush now, Honey."

Janet glanced at him. Their eyes met and she looked away. Jim knew that *lover* and *honey* had registered.

Well, let her stick up her nose until she snagged it on a cloud! What he needed was some sleep and some grub and a good shave. Yes, and time to let his bruises heal, also.

The fists and boots of the Big Boss' gang had not been very complimentary to his face.

The doc got to work with a towns-woman aiding him. The doc said, "All you bug-eyed bohunks git to hell outa here." Sheriff Albers herded the people outside, keeping an eye on Jim.

Outside Albers said, testily, "By hades, you'll never git a chance to kick me again!" and he took a swing at Jim.

Jim jumped back and ducked. "You're a brave son, Albers! If you feel so frosty why don't you tackle thet bunch of criminals up in Larb City?"

Somebody laughed.

"He's afeerd of them Larb City men," an old hag cackled. She showed toothless gums.

Albers said, "You shut up, Grandma Nippets."

Jim didn't want to go to jail. He knew that if he once got behind bars they might throw away the key. This Albers was no dumbell, he realized. Up in Larb City he had put on a friendly act; down here in Beaver Tail it was a different story, though.

Albers had tried to get across the impression he held no charge against him. Jim wondered, Where the heck is Bootjack? Was his friend in jail? By this time he should have contacted Jim.

"Don't order me aroun', Sher'ff Albers!"

Grandma Nippets had thin lips. And the bottom lip was set like a vise against the upper lip.

Jim measured the distance to his horse and judged it about a hundred feet. Grandma Nippets moved closer to him as she glared at Sheriff Albers. Before Grandma Nippets knew what had happened Jim had her around the waist. He swung her frail body in front of him to shield him.

His .45 was beside her, staring at Sheriff Mike Albers.

The suddenness of the move had caught the lawman off guard. Grandma Nippets kicked, tried to get loose, but Jim's arm held her securely. She was thin and wiry, and her body lacked the youthful softness of that of Vivie. Jim had to hang onto her or his goose was cooked.

"Be quiet, you ol' fool!" He snarled the words. "If you don't quiet down I'll let a bullet through you!"

He deliberately made his voice savage. He would not have shot the old woman under any circumstances, but Grandma did not know that. She gave out a big war-whoop of fear, then folded up in a faint. Which was just the way Jim wanted her—limp and resistless, yet making a good shield.

Jim started backing toward his horse. Grandma's heels dragged in the dust. Evidently a man behind Jim had pulled his gun for the sheriff said, "For hell's sake, Hank, don't shoot him from behin'! You'll ventilate Grandma, too!"

Jim grunted, "You use your head . . . sometimes, sheriff."

Albers stood helpless, .45 dangling from forefinger. Jim shot a glance at Janet. She watched silently. Their eyes met momentarily and Jim wondered just what her blue eyes—those china-blue eyes—held. But this question did not bother him long; his job was to get out of Beaver Tail, and get out right pronto.

The first element of surprise had died and now the townsmen watched him carefully as he backed toward his mount, gun up. They reminded him of a silent ring of wolves, seated on haunches, waiting for a misstep, a miscue. Then they would close in for the kill. He stumbled once, his heel hitting a rock, and one man moved a little, and Jim swung his gun on him, for he had hurriedly recovered his balance.

"Watch that paw of yours, son!"

The man's hand sprang back like it had a spring in it. His face showed a grin of fear that was almost foolish.

Jim reached his bronc. The old woman

was still out. Now came the real test. He had to drop the old woman and swing up fast and get out. His bronc, although tired, snorted a little, evidently awed by the strange spectacle of his master dragging along a woman old enough to be his grandmother.

Jim studied the silent, tense group, glanced at his bronc. Then suddenly he had dropped the old woman. His six-shooter sent dust lifting in front of the sheriff, who instinctively ducked. A few of the townsmen broke, and Jim's saddle came up and hit him between the legs.

He bent low over his bronc, riding backwards in his saddle, reins in one hand, gun in the other. The terrified horse stampeded, which was just what Jim wanted him to do.

Townsmen were scattering like sagehens running through sage ahead of a dog coyote who wanted a juicy breakfast. Sherriff Mike Albers had fallen on his belly. Gun braced across his forearm, he shot once. Jim's second lead threw more dust into the lawman's face.

Jim didn't want to hit him. He just wanted to scare him.

A bullet screeched overhead. Jim thought, That was a rifle, and he wished desperately that the bronc would reach the corner, turn it, and be out of sight. He glanced over his shoulder.

At this point the end of Beaver Tail's mainstreet ran into a building and the bronc would have to turn or crash into the hardware store. Jim judged the corner as being about three jumps away and then he turned his head back to watch the townsmen and the sheriff and Janet.

By this time, bullets were talking; Jim made a hard target though, for his horse was really running, jumping like a frightened jackrabbit. Jim felt him swerve, preparatory to swinging around the corner. Hope ran its length through the Texan's lanky frame. Once around that corner and a building would shield him for a few seconds.

Of course, there would be pursuit, and his cayuse was none too fresh, either. But once around the corner and he'd switch positions in his saddle and really use his hooks for speed.

The bronc swerved, hoofs raising dust. The corner suddenly jutted out and shut from view the men on the mainstreet. Jim heard their called curses and their noises; he put his hands on the seat of his kak, intending to swing his legs around so he could ride in the right manner.

He had gained his advantage: a few precious seconds of precious time. This thought was good, it was strong; he would be able to get back into the hills, look up his old friend Bootjack, work from the freedom and security of open range. His plan had worked—

Then it happened.

He got a glimpse of the kid. He was about ten or twelve years old—somewhere around that age—and he had a new catchrope. When Jim saw him he had just thrown out the loop, heading it for the front legs of Jim's bronc. The horse jumped to one side, but the noose settled; the kid frontfooted him perfectly. Jim glimpsed the kid taking dallies around a hitchingpost, and then his cayuse was going tail over tincup into the dust.

"I roped me a bandit!"

There was glee in the boy's voice but there was no happiness in the heart of Jim Carlin as he hit the dirt. He had his hands full for a few seconds. First he had to roll to one side, or else his bronc would have landed on him; second, he had to keep hold of his gun.

He managed to propel himself out of the saddle, landing on the right side of his horse, who landed on his back, saddle and all. The ground came up and hit him with a savage brutal blow. Jim tried desperately to hang onto his .45. But self preservation also demanded he break the impact of his skidding fall with both arms extended. The shock against his shoulder-blades was terrific. He rolled and skidded, skinning his forearms; in his thundering descent he somehow lost control of his gun. He had the dim, hazy recollection of it sliding out of reach; then he rolled over again, tasting dust.

There was irony in his thoughts, too.

Here he had evaded the sheriff and the mature townsmen, and a button had dumped him while he tried out his new lass rope. Jim glimpsed his bronc trying to get to his feet. But the rope still entangled the cayuse and he went down again in a flurry of dust. Jim tried to get to his feet, but the shock of his fall was thick in him. The dust was a gray, hanging screen, and he tried to get his gun. But another rope came in and settled around him before he, in his stunned condition, could see clearly.

"I roped him, men!"

It was the kid's voice again, hotly triumphant. Jim realized the youngster must have had two ropes. Jim turned and the kid jerked hard on the rope; Jim went down into the dust, the rope binding both ankles. The kid was dancing like a maniac on the end of the rope, hauling Jim away from his pistol.

They came around the corner then—Sheriff Albers and Janet and the others—and Jim could do nothing but sit there with his hands up and a foolish, dusty grin on his face as he waited for them.

The kid was hollering as wildly as a Sioux buck full of rotgut whiskey. "I kotched him, I looped him!"

"You sure did," Sheriff Albers said. He spoke to Jim. "Get to your feet an' git in front of my pistol. This time, sonny boy, you're goin' to the clink for sure."

Jim said, "I sure believe you, sher'ff."

12

JIM walked the length of his cell; this one was five paces long, not four like the sod shack back in Larb City. Also, it had more light in it, but what difference does sunshine make when a man's in jail?

He had had some tough luck. Dang that kid with the catchrope. There were a number of points that were far from clear. Of course, there was the riddle of the U U trailherd and of Rusty and old Pancho. He was no clearer on these matters, nor was he any closer to a conclusion, than when he and Bootjack had moved in on Hell Creek. He was a few days older, had more aches and pains, but he was darned little the wiser.

For one thing who had opened the door to the jailhouse over there in Larb City? Whoever he was he was plainly on the side of one Jim Carlin. Coincidence had also stuck up its fang-toothed head when he and Bootjack had almost been ridden down by the two holdup men who had robbed the clerk's office.

"How's the clerk, jailer?"

The old jailer looked up from his magazine. "He's gittin' along right well, I reckon." He looked down again. "No thanks to you, of course."

"How is Vivie?"

"Ain't answerin' no more questions. I'm hired by the county to stand guard over you an' not to answer your questions."

Jim's brows rose. "Oh, thanks a heap, sonny child."

An hour passed.

Janet Albers came down the corridor, her heels making sharp noises on the concrete, and Jim saw that she carried a tray covered with a white cloth. He got the welcome smell of hot coffee.

"Chuck, prisoner."

"The name," Jim corrected, "is not *prisoner*; it's Jim Carlin."

"It's *prisoner* to me!"

She kicked open the small steel-door at the bottom of the gate and shoved in the tray. Jim took it back to his bed.

Jim asked, "Where's my partner?"

"I don't know. My dad has had some men out trying to catch him, too. You did smart by sneaking into Larb City!"

"I'm guilty of no wrong. I'm innocent."

"They all are," she said stiffly. "When they get behind bars they're all innocent, or so they say. You must be quite a hand with the ladies, cowboy."

"Yeah, I've even kissed a deputy sheriff."

"Against her will, of course," she answered icily.

The jailer peered at them, specs high on his forehead. Janet turned and walked back to the office. This time her heels made even sharper and more strident noises. Jim admired her trim, straight back and found himself smiling. Then he looked at the curious face of the old jailer. His smile broke and turned sour.

"Mister, lookin' at you gives me the bellyache."

"You ain't so purty yorself, younker."

The meal was good. Jim found himself wondering if Janet had cooked it. If so she was a good cook; his old mother had always advised him to marry a good cook, too.

Despite his great hunger he ate rather slowly for the seriousness of his thoughts seemed to put a brake on the depth of his appetite. He had found out one thing for sure; Bootjack was still at large. The big man was luckier than he had been; at least, Bootjack enjoyed his freedom.

He still ached from his hard fall. But he had to grin as he remembered the exuberant kid spinning out that loop. Afterwards the kid admitted it had been the first time in his life he had ever front-footed a bronc. He had tried to rope them many times but had always failed until he had laid the noose in front of Jim's mount.

"I sure was lucky," the kid had piped. "First loop, too, and I got him. I dunno how I came to be packin' two ropes. Jus' decided I might need another. I was ridin' out to practice ropin sagebrush when I heard the hollerin' an' I piles off my bronc with my ropes—"

Jim shook his head sadly.

Around dusk Sheriff Albers came in, with Janet behind him. Bandits had stuck up a bank in Custer Bend, which was about a hundred miles south. One had been red-headed and the other had been a heavy-set fellow. He had got word from Custer Bend via the local stage driver.

"Sounds to me like they're the same gents that stuck up the clerk here," Jim ventured.

"Your old friends," Janet said sweetly.

Jim said, "What a knife you pack, sister!"

"Who are them two gents?" the sheriff wanted to know.

Jim shrugged. "If I knew them I'd go out after them. I'd drag them back an' make them confess that me an' my pard had nothin' to do with that clerk holdup.

How many charges you got against this Texas boy, nohow?"

Sheriff Albers recited them gravely. First, assisting bandits to hold up the office of the county clerk, which was armed robbery; second, jumping the posse, which, he claimed, was an offense —Jim couldn't see this but he did not argue. In fact, he only groaned. He was also accused of arson.

"Arson? That means burnin' down something, don't it?"

"You burned down the barn in Larb City."

Jim remembered that the old hostler's lantern had spilled kerosene all over the floor and had started to burn.

"I only hope no horses got burned."

"None did. One man got burned bad, though."

"Rather have him burned than to have an innocent bronc burn up." Jim looked at Janet. "What else against me?"

"Resisting arrest," the sheriff said. "Kidnappin' an ol' woman against her will." He screwed up his forehead in thought. "I reckon that's all."

"Assault and battery, too," Janet reminded. "He jumped you from behind back in that canyon."

"For Gawd's sake, woman, keep your mouth closed! I tol' you not to mention thet to nobody. What kind of a sheriff will they think I am if that word gets out?" He whirled on the old jailer. "You hear what she said?"

"Nope, boss."

"You'd better have not!" Albers was hotly serious. "If word gets out I'll lay it plumb on your shoulders an' off your soft job you go, understand?"

"I sure ain't heard nothin', sheriff."

Jim said dryly, "Thanks for reminding your father of that assault and battery charge, Janet. But don't mention it again or he'll blow his safety-valve and bust his boiler."

"Oh, shut up!"

Jim asked, "When do I get a trial, sheriff?"

"When I get damned good and ready to let you have one."

Sheriff Albers stalked away, his daughter following him.

Jim hollered, "That ain't what the law says. I'm supposed to find out what charges are against me in front of a justice of the peace—"

Bang!

The door rocked on its hinges.

Jim let go of the bars and walked to his bunk and sat down. The old jailer studied him as he chewed tobacco. Their eyes met and neither spoke. Finally the old man said, "A man will suffer lots of insults jes' to have a roof over his head an' a bellyfull of grub."

"And a jawful of tobacco," Jim growled. "Save your advice for some other poor sucker, gran' pa."

"They orta hang you," the old man retorted.

Jim leaned back on his pillow and laced his hands across the back of his skull. But his hands were skinned from his fall and his head ached more when he held it that way. He looked at the ceiling.

Unrest and dissatisfaction were living things inside of him that cried for freedom and for an answer. The red head and another man had held up the Custer Bend bank; perhaps that was why he had not seen Rusty in Larb City—Rusty had been out of the outlaw hangout on a raid? That was logical. He could do nothing in jail. Sheriff Albers was really mad and the lawman would see that the local J. P handed him plenty. Jim remembered the brutality of the Texas chain-gang. He wanted no more of bars. He decided he would die before he spent a term in prison.

But how would he get out?

Coldly he analyzed his prospects of breaking jail. Of course, there was old Bootjack—faithful old Bootjack—He was one ace in the hole. But Jim was sure that Sheriff Albers figured Bootjack might come to help him.

A day—a slow, dragging day—went by.

Restlessness became a trussed tiger in him, demanding freedom. He walked and walked, and his thoughts were terrible. He tested the steel bars of the single window but they were set deep into concrete. He doubted if a team of work-horses could have pulled them loose. He rattled the door until the old jailer cursed him in a shrill high tone.

Jim said, "Man, you amaze me! The sher'ff must've learned you how to cuss, the big bad man."

Sheriff Albers never came to see him during the day. At dusk Janet came with his tray from the Chinese cafe.

"How's Vivie?"

"You seem mighty interested in that cheap girl."

Jim shook his head. "She saved my life over in Larb City. She isn't cheap, Miss Janet. Sure, in the scale of things, she isn't much to reckon by, but she has a good kind heart, and that is a big thing. Not many people can compare with her that way."

She studied him, her eyes suddenly soft.

"Do you—love her?"

Jim shook his head again. "No, I don't love her, Miss Janet." The joking had left him and he was deadly serious. "I admire her for what she did for me, and I only hope she doesn't love me."

"What if she does? What will you do?"

"Please," he said, almost pleading. "Let me solve that, Janet. I have the answer now and to give it to you, if the word got to Vivie, would only hurt her, and she is so brave."

"Jim, I admire you."

"I hope you do, miss. That kiss I gave you in the canyon—well, I meant it, yes, but it was just impulse."

They were alone. She blushed and Jim liked her more than ever. "Oh, Jim, I don't know what to say."

He was very grave and very serious. "But you haven't told me how she is?"

Vivie was very sick, according to the doctor. Infection had set in and the long and jarring ride had weakened her through the exertion and loss of blood.

"She wants to see you, Jim. She calls for you."

"Could I—see her?"

"My father is out of—" She caught herself. Evidently she had made a slip and evidently she did not want him to know that her father was not in Beaver Tail town. He overlooked it. But still it registered. "I don't know, Jim."

"Call the jailer. He can hold a shotgun on me."

"Tomorrow, maybe."

Jim slept little that night. For one thing, he kept remembering Vivie; he saw her fall again in a dream, just as she had fallen in Larb City. For another thing, he kept thinking of Bootjack. Would he come? If he did come what would he do? They couldn't break out the bars because of the stiff concrete. Maybe Bootjack—if he did come—would only walk into a snare. He felt sure one reason they held him in jail was to get Bootjack James in Beaver Tail to try to free him, his partner.

Maybe even now guards were staked out around the jail waiting for Bootjack.

Jim thought, *I hope he stays away*.

Dawn seeped through the window, lay a blanket of light across his steel cot, and the light awakened him from a sound, short sleep—the sleep of utter exhaustion. He sat up and memory came back and the sourness came into him again, giving him a touch of bitterness alien to his character.

The jailer, silent and glum, gave him breakfast. Janet brought him dinner and he asked her again if he could see Vivie.

"She calls for you, the doctor says."

Jim pleaded to see her. Maybe if he talked with her she would get better—anyway she might feel better.

His words seemed to have an effect upon her. Her blue eyes were thoughtful, and they were on him; by now he knew she was more than interested in him. Little things, small incidents had told him that—the inflection on a word, the touch of her hand—brief though that touch had been—as he handed her his plate. She was the kind of woman he wanted but he did not tell her this. This was not the place nor was it the time, and he knew this.

"Will you be good, Jim?"

"I promise, girl." His smile was fleeting. "If it did any good, I'd say what we said when we were kids—not you and me, of course, as kids—but me an' my Texas friends. I'd say, 'I'll cross my heart and hope to die'."

She debated, head cocked. He got the impression that her assurance hid a cloak of nervousness. He did not know why he got that impression.

"All right, you've promised, Jim."

"Take the jailer with us."

"He's out to eat. You gave me your word. Your word is good with me."

Jim said, "I don't want you to get into trouble with your father."

"I'm a deputy," she reminded.

She unlocked the gate and Jim went down the corridor with the girl behind him. Sunlight felt good on his eyes; townspeople stared at them; they went to the hotel. She said, "Go up the stairs," and Jim tromped past the clerk and up the stairs. At the top she said, "Turn left. The room number is 9."

Jim found the room and knocked.

Maybe she had a gun in her hand, maybe she did not have. He had not looked back. He had given her his word.

"Come in."

A woman's voice, and it turned out that it belonged to the practical nurse. She too showed surprise. Vivie turned her head on her pillow and said, "Why, lover, you've come to see Vivie!"

Jim went to his knees beside her bed. Her slender bare arm came out and rested lightly across his shoulders.

"Jim, you should have left me in the badlands. Then you wouldn't have been in jail, lover."

His voice was thick with an emotion he could not hide. "Don't say that, honey. I'd die for you."

Her eyes searched his face. She let her arm drop and she breathed deeply and she closed her eyes.

"I believe that," she said.

She lay still waxen sick, very sick.

Jim stood up. He looked at Janet. She looked away. He saw she had tears and her bottom lip trembled.

Vivie said, without opening her eyes: "Kiss Vivie, Jim."

Again he looked at Janet. Not for permission but to see what she would do. She nodded.

Jim kissed the girl on the lips. Her lips were feverish and very dry.

The nurse said, "She's tired, and you must go."

Jim and Janet went outside. Outside in the hall Janet said, "Wait a minute, Jim."

Jim stopped. The hall was dark. He watched her.

"This town has sort of changed its mind about Jim Carlin," she told him. "When you brought Vivie back, knowing all the time you were going to jail—well, it changed a lot of minds, I understand."

Jim waited, silent, watching her.

"Even Dad—well, he isn't so sure of himself, either."

"I'm happy to hear that."

She continued, her voice low. "I've done some scouting on my own hook. I've contacted a man known as Bootjack James in the hills—"

"My partner." Jim said quietly.

"He's told me a lot about you and why you and he are up in this section. Jim, will you please go?"

He said nothing for a long moment. This had sort of stunned him, and the shock was a little too deep.

"You—you're turnin' me, a prisoner, loose?"

"You can put it that way, yes."

Jim shook his head. "I won't go, Janet."

"Why not?"

"It would put you behind the eight ball."

"Please, Jim."

For a moment the irony of this touched him. She was a deputy and he was a criminal and she was begging him to break jail!

"I won't do it," he repeated.

Behind him, from the door leading to a room, a familiar voice said, "Well, pard, if you wont go, then by hades I'll make you go."

Jim whirled, hand going to his hip; but his gun, of course, was not there. He stared at the man with open mouth.

Finally he said, "Bootjack, sure as hell. Bootjack."

"Get movin'," the grinning man said.

"Yes," Janet said, "make fast tracks. But wait a minute, men; tie me up first. Come into this room, quick, before somebody sees us all together!"

"We'll make it look like you got waylaid," Bootjack grinned. Then to Jim, "Her an' me arranged this."

Jim said, smilingly, "I'm not that dense, friend!"

13

JIM'S horse was behind the hotel, tied to a post in the alley. Jim grunted, "This is the bronc I had to leave in Larb City," and Bootjack said, "The sheriff had a man lead him into this burg."

"My gun, too," Jim said.

The gunbelt and the .45 were hung over the fork of his saddle. He went up and strapped on the weapon and the feel of it was good against his thigh. Beside him Bootjack swung his leg over his saddle with the easy gesture of a man who had seen a lot of miles with a horse between his legs.

"Your gun," Bootjack said.

Jim's bronc was fresh and he wanted to roll the cricket in his bit. Jim held his head high and turned him.

"We ride down this alley big as life," Jim said. "No loping or anything that will draw attention to us, savvy? We're jes' two waddies aheadin' back for camp."

"Jes' two innocent little cowboys," Bootjack said, smiling. "Thet deputy sure is a nice gal. I'd like to see her in front of my sink washin' dishes for me, Jim."

"You might see that yet."

Bootjack spat and said, "Fat chance, when I noticed the way she looked at you. Horse, step along light now, fella. Well, here we are at the end of the alley, an' open range is ahead."

Behind them a man hollered, "Hey, thet bandit is ridin' right out of town—there's the bandit—"

The sound of his six-shooter killed the rest of his words. Jim glanced back and saw a man, plainly drunk, back in the alley. The man wobbled on his feet and his aim must have wobbled, too, for Jim did not hear the whine of his bullet—it missed so far. Or maybe it was because his horse's hoofs were making so much noise; his horse was really stretching.

Bootjack hollered, "Bad luck!"

Jim made no answer. They were riding

so fast their broncs made so much noise that speech, if not impossible, was not so advisable.

And this situation needed no further discussion, Jim figured. Again Old Lady Luck had played a trump card against him and he only hoped she would soon be running out of cards. Tough luck was nothing new. Even a punk kid had front-footed his bronc and thereby had brought about a spell in the jail . . . and it had been the first horse the kid had ever frontfooted!

Behind them, he heard Beaver Tail come into life. Voices hollered and dogs barked and Smith's jackass broke out braying.

Bootjack reminded, loudly, "Sheriff ain't in town, Jim."

"Somebody'll get brave an' round up a posse. Wonder where Albers is?"

"I reckon he's out scoutin' aroun' for that red-head an' that other gent what robbed the Custer Bend Bank. Anyway, his daughter hinted at somethin' like that, only I didn't question her too close."

Jim had to smile. He remembered how foolish Deputy Sheriff Janet Albers had looked back in that hotel room when he and Bootjack had tied her to the bed post. Well, she'd made him look foolish almost every time they had met; now, he reckoned, it was her turn.

"Bootjack, two riders—over there!"

The pair had just loped around the base of a hill and they were about a hundred yards away. The two saw them and Jim saw them jerk in their broncs, sliding them to a halt in the loose shale.

"That's Jim Carlin, Ike; his pard is with him, too! Carlin's busted jail an '—"

Jim heard no more of Toad Graham's bellowing voice. His .45 talked loudly and killed the rest of the man's sentence. Jim had no hopes of connecting with a bullet; the distance was too far for short-gun work.

He glimpsed shale geysering upward in front of Big Ike Outland's rearing horse. Evidently the bullet slapped up some shale and it hit the horse in the belly and stung him with its sharp edges; anyway, the bay started to really buck.

Big Ike Outland had drawn his gun but he never got in a shot. He was hogging leather, both hands hooked around the saddle-horn as he lay back against the back of his saddle, trying to keep onboard.

"Whoa, you damn' knotheaded cayuse!"

The horse bucked into Toad Graham's mount. Toad's horse almost went down under the impact.

Jim grinned, blowing smoke from his weapon. The toe of a hill came out and seemed to pull him and Bootjack behind its protective barrier. They were in the rough country, and Jim figured they were safe by now. Luck had been with them for a brief period, and the Old Lady had slapped shale up against a horse, tying up Big Ike Outland and Toad Graham.

"Them two is jes' comin' in from Larb City," Bootjack hollered. "Well, here's where we leaves this trail, son."

"My horse is kinda winded."

"Foller me, child."

They rode through thick buckbrush, strong with its oily smells, and the trail widened. Behind them the buckbrush swished shut as though it were a door closing.

Jim's horse was breathing heavily. They were, he figured, about four or five miles from Beaver Tail town; the run had been made against a rising elevation and it had been a hard run. The bronc was not fagged out; he was just temporarily winded. He still had lots of possible miles in him but they would have to be made at a slower gait.

And right now he and Bootjack wanted speed, not endurance.

He knew that the citizens of Beaver Tail had organized a posse. Around every town, it seemed, there were some citizens who always rode in posses. That was because right before the posse would leave town the local saloons would load them up with free whiskey.

So far, they had seen no trace of a posse; neither, for that matter, had they seen anything more of the two O Bar O Connected men. Jim got the impression that Bootjack had planned their escape very diligently before making a deal with Janet Albers.

"Hope we don't run across nobody else," Jim said; "my cayuse is almost down on his knees."

"We'll fix that. Here's the clearin', Jim. Get down an' unsaddle an' take that gray hoss there."

A gray and a blue roan were in the clearing, tied to picket-pins. Jim went down and he said, "You've missed nothin', friend. I see these broncs pack the O Bar O Connected, an' I figure you stole them from Big Ike, eh?"

"Stole them!" Bootjack repeated the words in a hurt tone. "Me. I never steal nothin', I jes' borrowed them broncs!"

Jim peeled the saddle from his horse and stripped the ear-split bridle headstall from his sweaty head. He slapped the bronc on the rump and the horse trotted to a spring that had made a little pool of water against the far bank of the canyon.

He got the hackamore rope and pulled the gray in, with the horse snorting against such rough treatment. But this was no time or place to cater to the whims of a strange horse. He jammed the bit between grass-stained teeth and got the animal's right ear through the ear-hole in the headstall.

"Take it easy, pony."

Bootjack grinned as he swung up his saddle. The kak landed and the big man caught the cinch as it swung under the horse's belly.

"Whoa, boy."

Bootjack's pony was skittish. Jim saw the big man take the horse's head in his two immense hands and he saw him twist the bronc around bodily. It was a feat of terrible strength, almost bringing the big horse to his knees; and when the horse was released all desire to scrap seemed to have left him.

"Now be a good hoss, eh?"

Jim neckreined his horse around. "He'll be good."

Bootjack lifted his leg and landed in his

leather. "Me, I'd like to do that to Toad Graham's neck. Only I'm afraid I might bust it."

"Would that be too bad?" Jim asked.

A shake of the heavy head. "Not too bad, at that. Jim, you notice back yonder that Graham had a hard time gettin' his gun from leather? Odd thing, but I noticed he dropped his reins, then reached for his pistol."

"He had a bum arm," Jim said. "He could only use his good hand."

"Anythin' in that, Jim?"

Jim gave this some thought as they rode out of the clearing, leaving their tired horses behind. He remembered that he had shot a man when he had escaped from the Big Boss' cabin back in Larb City and at that time he had noticed that the man had been as big as Toad Graham, and that the resemblance despite the darkness had been rather close.

He told Bootjack this.

The big man cocked his head and his heavy thumb stroked his bottom lip. Finally he said, "Maybe we're readin' somethin' into this thet might not be there. Maybe Toad just dropped his reins in his excitement. We must have give that pair a bad shock, ridin' right smack-dab onto them that way."

Jim nodded.

The ground lifted finally, rising gradually to a slope on which scrub pine and ground-juniper grew. They reached the summit and there they looked back of them. Jim was the first to see the group of riders moving toward the east. They were about four miles away and they rode at no great haste.

"Townsmen from Beaver Tail," he commented.

Bootjack said, "Way off the trail. Nursin' their free bottles, I guess. Wonder where Graham an' Big Ike is?"

Jim took his field-glasses from his saddlebag and the glasses moved slowly in a semi-circle. He found a spot and took a close scrutiny of it; this location was almost in Beaver Tail.

"There they are."

Bootjack took the glasses and fitted and

adjusted them. "Ridin' out of the brush for town. Reckon they met that so-called posse and still didn't ride with 'em?"

Jim nodded.

Bootjack handed back the glasses.

Jim said, "Big Ike is smart. All right, fella, where have you been, an' what's happened since I headed out for Larb City?"

A lot had happened, it turned out. Bootjack gave the news to his partner in just a few words for his vocabulary and his time were limited. Big Ike Outland had sent over two punchers and they had burned Jim's outfit to the ground over on the land which Jim had homesteaded.

"They done run me off 'n the rimrock, Jim. I stung one with a rifle ball but didn't hurt him bad, I reckon. They stampeded our team an' raised hell in general."

"You sure they were Outland hands?"

"They rode out from the O Bar O Connected. An' who else would hit at our junk on the homestead?"

"Nobody else."

Bootjack gave his boss a slanting inquisitive look. "You still aim to hang onto that homestead?"

Jim did.

"Why?"

Jim had a reason—a couple of reasons, in fact. One was that it was time he settled down; the other had lovely blonde hair, she was built just right in the right places, and she had clear blue eyes. She also packed a deputy-sheriff's star—that is, she had packed one, until he had lifted it. Some day he'd give her badge back. He'd take it out of its cache and deliver it to her. But first he had some items to tend to.

He only gave his partner the first reason.

Bootjack said slowly, "Odd, how a man gets an idea he *has* to settle down. Maybe he reads that some place in some stuff put out by the banks. They want a man to tie hisself down to a lot of property so they can get him in debt and have him work for them all the time for nothin'."

"Then what did you do?" Jim wanted

to switch the topic of discussion to some less touchy point.

Bootjack had even ridden into Larb City, being worried about Jim. There assailants had jumped him in a dark alley but he through sheer brawn had beaten them off. Then he had heard about Jim riding into town with Vivie and about Jim being jailed.

"Thet deputy sheriff—thet female one —she tol' me."

Jim waited, smiling.

"She's loco about you. She was worried sick."

"Glad to hear that."

Bootjack looked sadly at him.

"A woman always splits up two men. An' I *used* to have such a danged good pardner, too!"

Jim only smiled wider.

14

THEY sat on a bluff and talked. Behind them their saddlers grazed in the grass, eating with their bits in their mouths, for their masters were taking no chances—they might have to get out in a hurry. The broncs made noises as they chewed, and occasionally one or both would stomp at heelflies.

Jim watched the shadows gather in their majestic splendor as they bathed the range-country with their darkness. He had always liked the evening and the dusk; now, sitting on this rimrock bluff, he had an eagle's view of this land below. And he liked what he saw.

For one thing the land reminded him remotely of his old Texas home with its rolling hills and its coulees thick with brush. Only these hills were higher and more rocky and rough; the buckbrush in the coulees was not as thick as the chaparral of the Lone Star State. A moment of reverence held him as he worshipped at God's outdoor chapel. The sun was falling and the land looked soft and quiet and calm, the saffron shadows enclosing this wide country. Yes, the land looked calm; yet, under its quietness, the cowboy knew there was danger.

Danger against him, and danger against Bootjack.

"Yonder is Milk River," Bootjack said, and his forefinger pointed. "Kinda reminds a man a mite of the ol' Pecos, eh?"

Jim looked, and nodded.

Bootjack slapped at a mosquito. "We've been on this land for quite a spell, Jim. So far we've found no sign of where the U U herd went. I talked with a waddy a few days ago an' I mentioned kinda casual like that down in Texas I punched cows for an outfit called the U U"

"Yeah?"

"He looked at me an' said he didn't know that iron. Maybe I'm wrong but it sure seemed as though he was hidin' somethin'."

"Them cattle came into this country," Jim allowed. "Then they just plumb disappeared. I'm purty sure that redhead was Rusty. Thet horse that toted him was Sonny. He's fast, that Sonny; he's got bottom, too, for a long hard ride. If I was holdin' up a bank I'd sure cotton to swing a leg over Sonny fer a getaway bronc."

Bootjack nodded. He added that surely Rusty must have heard they were in this section of Montana—they'd raised enough Cain in the few days they had been in this area.

All this time, Jim had had a gnawing fear in him. At first the cause of it had been uncertain but gradually the root of it had become clear. This root had twisted into his thoughts like an insidious thread of danger and distrust and now it almost made him groan in anguish.

Bootjack looked at him. For some moments his very large and kindly eyes were on his partner.

Then he said, "I know what you're thinkin', Jimmy boy."

This time Jim Carlin did groan. "Gawd, Bootjack, would Rusty do that to us? Would he highjack our herd and sell it an' go on the outlaw trail?"

"I hope not."

Jim pulled a dried blade of grass free and chewed on it to hide his emotions. He looked out over the basin for a long moment and he was silent. Down in Beaver Tail town, miles away, lights were going on; they were fireflies lighting the flatlands, and distance made them twinkle. But his eyes were no longer on the beauties of this Montana dusk.

"He knew what that herd meant to us. He knew that it meant a new start for us, a promise to make a good livin' honestly on clean range and free grass."

"He's your brother," Bootjack pointed out.

Jim looked sharply at him. "What man knows his brother? Even though he was raised side by side with him."

"I agree with you there."

Jim said, "Where is Pancho Torres?"

"I've heard scattered talk about a gent they call the Wild Man."

Jim nodded.

Bootjack asked, "Well, Jim, what is the answer?"

"I don't know. We got to act a lot on what we think an' on hunches. I got a hunch that the O Bar O Connected is tied into this. I told you about my meetin '—if it could be called that—with the Big Boss. His voice came through a tube, it sounded like. That hid his voice. But I'm danged sure I shot Toad Graham when I busted out of that Larb City clink with Vivie."

"But you're not sure."

"No, and I don't know who t'hell let me out of there."

Bootjack asked, "What's next?"

Jim got to his feet. "We ride for the O Bar O Connected. That's the best thing to do now."

"Good idea."

The O Bar O Connected was an outfit of many buildings—most of them made of native cottonwood logs—and it lay sprawled along the dark base of a high butte that threw shadows across the buildings, giving them an ominous appearance. The road came along a small creek, twisting like a tired rattlesnake, and then it crossed this creek by a wooden bridge, the planks of this being worn splintery and rough by the gouging of horse-shoes.

Jim Carlin had correctly gauged the ruthlessness of Big Ike Outland, and by these tokens cold logic had told him the outfit would have a guard out. Guinea hens, he noticed, roosted on corral bars and in cottonwood trees, and guinea hens, he knew, had watchdogs beaten as guards. Let a strange noise occur and the hens would raise their raucous racket.

Had he not known that Big Ike was a former Texan, he would have known it now because of the guinea hens; his own Texas home, during Indian trouble, had used guinea hens as watchdogs. But after the redskins had settled down on reservations his father had abandoned the use of guinea hens, for the birds were naturally noisy. He knew that Big Ike expected trouble of some sort or the hens would not have been in evidence. Or did their presence bespeak of a guilty conscience?

He and Bootjack, before riding to the big outfit, had shot another O Bar O Connected cow. They had skinned the area around the brand and scraped the hide but had found no trace of the U U iron. This was confusing. If the O Bar O Connected had rustled the herd and rebranded it, then why did not the old brands show through? Or had Chance made them shoot two cows originally branded with the O Bar O Connected?

He realized they were working a lot on guesswork. But what other resource had they upon which to depend?

That was the irony, the bitterness, of this whole affair. He was a hunted man now, the law wanted him; only because of a golden-haired girl was he free—and in freeing him she had turned against her father. This was not good; there was no meat in this; the strength was missing.

But his thoughts were dangerous things; he put them into the discard. He had only the present. The past was dead and the future was uncertain. And where was Rusty?

Maybe Rusty was dead, maybe—No, there was the redhead riding out of Beaver Tail, and he had been astraddle the buckskin named Sonny. Jim shook his head. He looked at the big honest face of his faithful friend.

"Yonder's the guard in thet buck-brush?"

Bootjack squinted. "Where?"

Jim pointed. Bootjack said, "My eyes ain't as good as they used to be. I've been readin' the fine print on too many wanted-man dodgers. You know, they already got them printed about us; read one on a post yesterday."

"Bad luck," Jim said. "All you bring is bad luck."

"I'll bring bad luck to that guard."

Bootjack went through the brush. Within fifteen minutes he was back. He toted the limp form of the guard over his shoulder and he dumped him unceremoniously onto the ground, disregarding the fact that the guard's head hit a rock. Jim looked at the man who lay unconscious, neck twisted.

"Mebbe you busted his neck, you big ox!"

"Nah, it's still one, although it is warped a little."

"He'll sleep for some time," Jim said, "but it's best we tie an' gag him. Use his belt and his neckscarf an' his bandanna."

The guinea hens cackled as they came in through the brush. After a while the bunkhouse door opened and a man appeared limned against the lamp light.

"Damn those damned hens!"

"They must sniff a coyote," a voice behind him said. "They're always cacklin'. If 'n it ain't a c'yote it's a wolf or a weasel tryin' to suck their blood—wish t'hell a mink would come along an' kill them all off. A mink'd get 'em for sure."

"Wonder if they's somethin' wrong?"

"Nothin wrong. Prob'ly the boss an'

Toad comin' back from town. If they was somethin' wrong Charlie'd warn us."

The bunk house door slammed shut.

Jim said, "I didn't hear it all but it seemed as though I heard him say the boss an' Toad was still in town."

"You heard right."

Jim said, "We gotta get Toad."

"We're here, so let's look aroun'."

The back door of the big ranch-house was unlocked. They scouted around it, found nothing; Jim felt a moment of loss. He did not know just what to expect to find in the ranch-house, if anything. Then he had an idea.

"Go to the barn, Bootjack, an' see if Sonny is in with the hosses."

"Good idea."

"I'll meet you at our broncs."

Bootjack peered at him through the encroaching darkness. "You got somethin' on your mind," he accused.

"Jes' like a naggin' woman," Jim said.

Bootjack said, "Meet you at the broncs," and went out the back door. Jim pushed the table against the wall and put chairs around it. Then he got some kindling from the fireplace. He pulled down all the blinds and then crumpled a newspaper and put it under the kindling. His match made a dancing, merry light. The kindling came to flame and the chairs started to burn. Soon the wall was on fire. The blinds still hid the fire from any possible viewer on the outside; yes, and the men were all in the bunkhouse.

Hastily he opened wide those windows that were in the rear of the house and that could not be seen from the bunkhouse. By this time the fire had gained headway; the heat was growing intense. When he left he opened the rear door wide to give the fire an added draft.

He climbed the hill, moving through scattered clumps of buckbrush. Close to the summit, he suddenly stopped.

A noise up ahead.

He glimpsed a dim form leaping buckbrush and he recognized a mule-tail deer; the tension left his wiry frame. By the time he had reached their horses, the house below was burning rapidly; so far, the men in the bunkhouse had not noticed it, either.

Bootjack was not with their horses.

He waited.

Bootjack finally came out of the buckbrush. "I looked at their horses. Sonny wasn't there. Not a buckskin in their *remuda*."

"The house is on fire. It accidentally caught on fire, I guess."

"I noticed that."

They waited and soon a voice hollered, "Hell, men, look at the house burn!" and in the scarlet light they saw men run out of the bunkhouse. Down there on the basin floor, moving through the red uncertain light, they looked like pygmies, running back and forth.

"Start a bucket brigade from the pump!"

"Man, will the boss be mad!"

15

TOAD GRAHAM was having tough luck. Although he had held good hands, somebody else had always had a better hand. Pot after pot had been lost because of this fact.

He leaned back in his chair and squinted at his cards. "I'll raise you five, Big Ike."

"Called."

A man came in and said, "Toad, is that your sorrel tied out behind?"

"Yeah, that's my bronc."

"I was just out to the backhouse," the man said, sitting down. "Thet sorrel is goin' loco. He's tryin' to rear up even though he is tied down. Hear him strike at the post?"

"What's wrong with him?"

"I dunno. I want no part of a bad hoss. But he might break loose his reins an' run off on you."

"He's tied with a hackamore rope."

"Might get his front feet over the rope an' hang hisself up. Who's the bettor, an' what's the deal, men?"

"Hold up," Toad Graham grunted angrily. "I'm goin' out an' work thet bronc over." He waddled toward the rear door.

"Don't let him work you," a man advised, winking at Big Ike Outland. "Wonder when thet posse'll head back into town?"

"When they run outa whiskey," a man grunted.

The door slammed shut behind Toad Graham. True to the man's prediction, the horse was rearing and fighting. Toad grunted, "Now what the hell is wrong with him?" for the sorrel was a well-broken horse of eight years old. Toad didn't know that Jim Carlin had put a lighted cigar butt under the bronc's saddle blanket. Jim had hated to hurt the horse but he wanted to get Toad out into the open and this seemed the best way to bring this about.

The lamplight from the saloon, coming gingerly through a rear window clothed with cobwebs, showed that the horse had hooked a front leg over the hackamore rope. He was struggling to get free and in his struggles he was choking himself.

Toad said, "Pony. I'll beat you—"

His words were choked off suddenly. They did not even have time to die in a gurgle; they were immediately shut off. Toad felt a huge set of hands come around his neck and they were like steel clamps. His head went to one side and blackness came in, and he could only hit with his one hand. He tried to twist around to see who held him but this failed and then something round came down across his skull.

Toad Graham's giant knees gave way.

"Drag him over here," Jim whispered. He holstered his gun. "You ain't got the strength in your hands that you used to have."

"I'm gettin' old, I reckon."

"Dump him against this shed."

Toad Graham's slack body landed on

the ground. Jim used his jackknife to cut open the big man's shirt. He found Graham's bandages and tore them loose. Finally his fingers told him he had the man's skin bare.

"Light a match, quick."

The match flared, and showed a wound in the man's shoulder. Jim got a glimpse of it and then Bootjack killed the match. They both stood up. Below them Graham breathed with a calm, cowlike breathing.

"A bullet hole," Jim said quietly.

"A bullet hole," Bootjack confirmed.

Jim said, "We'd best get out of town."

They had hidden their horses along Beaver Creek and had walked the short distance into town. This was better than riding in, they had figured. As Jim walked past the sorrel he cut the hackamore rope. The horse trotted away. He did not buck now and Jim figured the cigar had gone cold.

They got to their broncs without mishap. Jim had the ironical thought that this was the first time they had left town without trouble.

Bootjack asked, "Well, what's next?"

Jim squatted on his heels and contemplated the question. Out to the west a cow bawled and finally a calf answered. These, then, were the night's only sounds. He looked up at his pard.

"Well, he had a bullet-hole in his shoulder, and the bandage was a patched-up affair—evidently not put there by a doctor."

"I noticed that."

Jim said, "He might have been the guy I winged, at that." He stood up. "He has to be the gent. Same build and a bullet hole . . . Well, that ties Graham into the Larb City bunch, but what about his boss?"

"If he's in it, then Big Ike is in it, too. That's only logical, it is."

Jim conceded that.

"Well," Bootjack asked, "what is the next card?"

Jim said. "I gotta talk with Sheriff Albers."

"About what?"

"About Rusty, of course. And the

herd, too. He should know somethin'. So far we've acted on the quiet, we have. Now we got to tip our hand to the sheriff."

"He might be in with Big Ike and Graham."

"I doubt that."

"Don't let thet girl's purty face turn your logic, Jim."

"I won't."

"I'd like to be sure of that."

Jim spoke angrily. "Damn it, man, I've got my right senses, an' I'm over twenty-one, too! Now don't rile me no longer!"

Because of the darkness Jim could not see the smile on Bootjack's big face but he caught the man's chuckle.

"Jes' sandpaperin' you, pard."

Jim felt regret for his hasty temper. "Come along," he said gruffly. "You might come in handy."

"I might . . . at that."

Sheriff Mike Albers and his wife and daughter lived on the outskirts of Beaver

Tail, in a small coulee west of the town that squatted on the mesa and overlooked the Beaver Creek valley. The sheriff was an old time cowboy and he always liked to putter around and raise a few steers each fall. He would butcher them and then sell the meat to townspeople.

He had a dog but the animal seemed very friendly. He came up to Jim and he wagged his tail and he wanted to lick the cowboy's face. Jim said, "Nice boy," and the dog wagged so hard he threatened to throw his spinal column out of alignment.

"The kind of dog I like," Bootjack said.

The sheriff was sitting at the table. Bootjack and Jim squinted through the window. Mrs. Albers was beside the fireplace, knitting; Janet was nowhere in sight.

Bootjack murmured, "Wonder where the gal is?"

"Prob'ly down to the office. She's a deputy, you know."

"Political drag an' graft! She ain't one

to tote a star an' a gun. She oughta be washin' diapers, she should."

"Listen to who's talkin'," Jim whispered.

Bootjack said, "He's a-studyin' want-dodgers, ain't he? Them cardboards has pictures on them." He chuckled silently. "They all ain't got no pictures of us, they ain't. Jes' some words about us."

"That's enough."

Bootjack drew back away from the window but Jim had a quick study of Mrs. Albers. She was as small as Janet, and her hair was now grey; still, her body held good lines, and she was a stylish, pert woman.

Janet, he figured, would be like her mother, when she got that age. Jim spoke to his partner.

"His gun an' belt is hangin' on the wall hook an' must be twenty feet away from him. The closest weapon is a rifle in the gunrack against the near wall."

"Maybe his wife totes a pistol."

"Oh, act sensible."

"There's nothin' wrong with that, is

there? His daughter totes a pistol. Like daughter like mother, they say."

"You got it backwards," Jim said. "Cover me from the window, eh?"

"All right."

Bootjack went back to the window. Jim and the dog went to the front door. Jim swallowed twice, for he did not like this; still, it had to be done. He knocked and without waiting for a reply he stepped into the room. He did not pull his Colt, but he kept his hand on its handle.

"Folks, stay just where you are!"

His entrance had been rather dramatic, he had to allow. Mrs. Albers stared, knitting needles stilled, and he noticed that her jaw became very stiff. Her husband held a want placard in mid air, staring at him.

"Well, I'll be—It's Jim Carlin, mother."

"What do you mean by entering our home like this?" the woman said angrily.

Jim said, "I'm a wanted man, and I had to be sure I was safe. I only want to ask your husband a few questions."

"I don't like your rude entrance, sir."

"Neither do I, but it is necessary."

"I—"

"Sorry, madam," Jim spoke to the sheriff. "Sir, I've got important business."

"Spit it out."

"I made a mistake when I came into town. I filed on a homestead and used my real name."

"I don't follow you, Carlin."

Jim told the lawman about Rusty Carlin and the missing U U trailherd. "Rusty was my brother. I owned one-half of the herd. The other half belonged to Rusty and Bootjack, my partner."

While he talked he watched the lawman closely. But the sad, glum face of Sheriff Mike Albers showed nothing. It was, in fact, like an emotionless bunch of weather-beaten rock, and only the eyes seemed alive as they watched him closely.

"I know nothing about your herd, Carlin. But I understand this redheaded bandit is known as Rusty."

Jim felt his spirits sag. "Do you know his last name?"

"I've never heard it."

Jim nodded. "Well, that's the deal, sheriff. I had to talk it over with you so you could see where I stand and I thought perhaps you had some information for me. But I see you ain't got none. Who's this gent they call the Big Boss?"

"I've heard of him. I don't know his identity."

"Who is the gent they call the Wild Man?"

Albers' eyes were heavy with something Jim could not understand. Finally he pegged it as just plain bewilderment. Or was it that? This lawman was a tough page to attempt to read.

"You got me on that, Carlin. He came into this country about a year ago, or around that time, an' he lives back in the hills. He never has come into town. Some claim he's plumb loco, others say he's jes' a hermit."

"You ever see him?"

"Only from a distance an' then through

fieldglasses. He eats off the lan' an' lives back in the Larb Crick rough country. Eli Jones leaves a handful of salt every month or so on a rock back there an' he must come after it 'cause it's always gone in a few days."

"What did he look like?"

"Why you so interested in that loco gent?"

"That's my business, sheriff. I asked you what he looked like." Mrs. Albers' gaze settled on her husband. Jim was getting impatient to leave. He had been in this house long enough and he did not like the circumstances.

"Wahl, he looked dark, he did; kinda like mebbe he was a Mex, or mebbe a 'breed. But his hair was long an' he was a distance off—"

Jim said, "Thanks, sheriff." He backed toward the door. "There'll be no use tryin' to do any trackin' after me. The night is kinda dark an' I ride a fast horse."

Albers said. "I'll pick you up later."

"You sound sure of yourself."

"I am. You'll make an error."

Jim said, "Good night, Mrs. Albers."

The matron snorted. "Good night shirt, outlaw! The nerve of you sayin' *good night* like that—after tyin' up my daughter after you talked her into lettin' you visit with a dancehall hussy!"

Jim realized this old girl was a tough nut to crack. And his smile was not pleasant as he backed out the door.

16

JIM ran for his horse and found his stirrup and rose. Already Bootjack was heading down the trail and the sound of his hoofs was rising against the night. Jim figured that Sheriff Mike Albers would make no attempt to follow them. The night was too dark, for one thing.

He caught up with Bootjack.

They almost ran over the rider. The rider came at a walk and therefore his gait made no noise. One minute the trail was clear ahead; the next a rider and mount was in it.

Bootjack grunted, "Ride 'im down!"

Jim had his .45 in his hand. Then he recognized the rider and he jerked his mount around and said, "Miss Janet, sure as shootin'!"

"Jim Carlin! Now what trouble are you in?"

Jim said, "Do I have to be in trouble?"

"You got me into enough trouble," the girl said. "I-I lost my job because I got soft-hearted and let you escape! Dad—fired me! All because of a no-good cowboy who worked on my sympathy!"

She slapped him squarely across the face.

Jim was really taken aback. First there was surprise; this was replaced by the age-old question of, *What man can ever understand a woman?* She had a hefty swing; the smarting of his jaw told him that.

"You thought of it."

"I must've been—mad! Or crazy!"

Jim said, "You're actin' kinda loco now, ain't you?"

"Get out of my sight!"

"With pleasure, honey! But first—"

Their horses were shoulder to shoulder. She started to say something but Jim's embrace and his rough, hurried kiss stopped her words. She struggled, her breast pushing against him, and the clean, fine feel of her was strong in his grasp.

His lips were clumsy. For one thing, the night was too dark; for another, his attack—and it could almost be called just that—had been too abrupt.

"Damn you, Jim Carlin, I'll—"

Jim shouted back, "You'll do nothin', Janet." His spurs lifted and his bronc went ahead.

Bootjack said, "She might have a gun, fella."

Jim shook his head. "She did have but she ain't got it now. When I kiss them I lift their guns!"

He waved Janet's .38.

"Well, I'll be danged," Bootjack grunted.

The darkness hid Jim Carlin's smile. Had it been daylight Bootjack would have noticed it was not a happy smile. For Jim was remembering Janet's hasty, hot-tempered words; she, too, had turned against him. That was not a pleasant thought. He decided again that women were a riddle to him. Why she should suddenly become angry with him was beyond his comprehension. She had been the one to think of the jail delivery scheme. Just because it had backfired and hurt her was no reason she should be angry with him. She had hatched the plan; not he.

He thought, *I'll have to do some explainin' to get back into her good graces*, and he wondered, briefly, if he would ever get back into her favor. But this thought was not long with him. Another supplanted it: He had lifted her badge, first; now he had her pistol.

But she had sure acted out of character, he figured. He put his bronc even with that of his partner.

"Where now?" Bootjack hollered.

"We find the Wild Man."

"An' that," hollered Bootjack James, "might be quite a chore to do!"

When dawn came they rode down off the rim rock and came to Larb Creek. They were about twenty five miles south of Beaver Tail. They rode into the yard of Eli Jones' outfit just as that rawboned individual was milking his cow.

"Howdy, cowboys."

Jim said, "I'm Jim Carlin; this gent is my pard, Bootjack James. Understand you're Eli Jones?"

"I am." Shifty eyes peered up at them out of a long face that sported sandy colored whiskers. "You gents ain't got no bone to pick with me, is you? Heck, I'm jes' a harmless shirt-tail cowman with a few head of dogies, tryin' to make a livin' for me an' my woman an' young uns. I've had nothin' but trouble from the O Bar O Connected an' I wants no more."

Jim almost smiled. But he assured Eli Jones that he and Bootjack came not for trouble but for information.

"I'll sure supply it if 'n I kin, men. I've heerd about you two. Posse went through last night lookin' for you. Mite near every one of them boys was so drunk they couldn't hang to their saddles. One fell right off'n his cayuse out in my yard. I helps him up an' the missus says, says she—"

Jim cut in with, "You put out salt for the Wild Man. He comes in an' gets it.

We want to talk to the Wild Man. Where do you put the salt?"

"If you kin blab with him, men, you got me beat. I've never bin able to make a conflab with him yet, an' I've tried."

Jim was interested in this phase of the conversation. Eli Jones had tried to track down the Wild Man. His reward had been bullets placed so closely to him that they had over-ruled his curiosity.

"He sure is a good shot with a rifle. I don't know where he gets his powder an' balls. He shoots jes' close enough to me to turn me back. From what I hear Big Ike Outland has tried to kill him."

"Why?"

Eli Jones squirted milk at the cat who sat a few feet away. The cat was just in the act of opening his mouth to meow. The milk hit him right in the mouth, which was just what the cat wanted. Jones returned his attention to his milk pail.

"Big Ike claims this Wild Man is livin' off'n O Bar O Connected beef. There's somethin' fishy about that Wild Man. He came in here jes' a few months ago. Somebody claims he tried to kill Big Ike. They say he shot Big Ike from his horse about four months ago, in the winter."

Jim nodded.

"That's all I know," Eli Jones said.

Jim and his partner mounted. Jim glanced significantly at the house. Eli Jones read the purpose of the glance.

"Mazie wife, don't raise a rifle ag'in these men, kase they don't aim to do us no harm."

Silence.

"You hear me, you danged woman?" Eli Jones cursed his wife.

From inside the house a whining feminine voice said, "All right, dad."

Eli Jones untied his cow. "She's a stubborn heifer, thet woman of mine, but she's honest, an' thet means a lot. You men can ride out without no trouble."

Jim said, "Bootjack, ride into the brush. I stay here an' cover you. Then you cover me."

Bootjack rode into the buckbrush along Larb Creek. Jim watched the house, gun in hand.

"Ain't no call for such precautions," Eli Jones whined. Jim merely nodded.

Bootjack called, "I'm stationed, Jim. Ride out."

Jones said, "Oh, yes, another thing, Carlin. A fella rode through here last night hell a-goggin' an' said somebody had burned down the O Bar O Connected house."

"You don't say!"

"Tried to lay the blame on me, he did, but shucks, my only hoss was in the barn bone dry an' without sweat on him, an' I'd been under sougans for a hour, anyway. Then this fella headed for town. Along about this mornin' another hand came through an' said thugs had beat up on Toad Graham down in Beaver Tail."

"News to me," Jim said.

Eli Jones' narrow eyes twinkled. "Thanks, Carlin," he said. He picked up his milk pail and went toward the house. He stopped once and looked back. "You'll find thet rock out in the rough country. You cain't miss it. Like I done tol' you you rides alone a coulee an' there's a lone boxelder at its end an' the rock is above that—shucks, a man can see it for miles. Injuns call it Flathead Rock kase it's right flat on top. Sandstone, it is."

Bootjack said, "Come on, son, an' get out of here!"

Jim said, "Thanks, Jones," and turned his bronc.

They loped through the brush and the cottonwood trees and boxelders hid them from the house. Through the protective cover they rode about two miles and then they left the creek bottom with its tall grass and swampy smells and angled into the hills that flanked the narrow valley. They rode up an incline and from its summit they could see the tips of the Little Rocky Mountains to the southwest, gaunt and lonely and blue against the sun's early color. To the south were the Piney Hills, and Larb City was in those hills. Jim figured that Larb City knew where Rusty was, but Larb City might never tell. But it seemed illogical that an entire trailherd and its two drivers could so utterly and completely disappear. Very illogical, he reasoned.

He remembered the strange look that had come into Sheriff Albers' eyes when he had mentioned the lost U U trailherd. Was the sheriff in on this deal? He did not like this thought because it reflected back on Janet, but there was this possibility; he could not ignore it. Other lawmen in other sections had worked with outlaws. Yet he hoped this were not true.

Somebody on this range knew about the U U trailherd and that somebody knew what had become of the herd. So far he hadn't talked to that party. He only hoped that the Wild Man turned out to be none other than old Pancho Torres. But this was an illogical thought, too.

Or was it? He gave it deep scrutiny. It seemed to him that old Pancho, upon hearing that Jim Carlin and Bootjack were in this country, would immediately look him up. He played with this presumption. He found its answer; that answer was simple.

The Wild Man, if he were Pancho

Torres, would have no way of knowing that he and Bootjack were in this Beaver Tail country, for from what he had heard nobody got to talk to the Wild Man. Bullets kept all intruders a safe distance away.

"You figger this Wild Man could be Pancho?" Bootjack twisted on his stirrups and looked at him.

"Might be," Jim said. "Let's hope so, pard. 'Cause if he is Pancho he can clear this up. I'd've looked for him before but I never knew until today where we might have a chance of locatin' him."

"Yeah, an' we've been powerful busy, too."

Jim smiled. "We might get busier," he admitted.

They rode ahead, the sunlight running across the hills, the wind talking through the pine trees. Jim was trying to fit the Big Boss' voice into some familiar niche in his mind. But the voice had been so disguised he could not find a spot for it in his memory.

The wound on Toad Graham had told

him definitely his hunch had been correct. He had shot Toad Graham the night he and Vivie had escaped from the Larb City sod shack.

One thing fitted against another. Toad Graham worked for Big Ike Outland. Toad worked for the Big Boss; otherwise, he would not have shot at Jim; otherwise, Toad Graham would not have been in Larb City.

Was Big Ike Outland the Big Boss?

17

THE sun was noon-high when they came to the flat sandstone rock. True to the words of Eli Jones the rock could be seen for a long distance. They had raided a line-camp and got some salt. Evidently the line-camp belonged to the O Bar O Connected outfit, for that outfit's brand had been burned into the log door. They took all the grub out of the camp and then burned it.

"We'll get even for Outland burnin' our outfit," Bootjack grunted.

Jim smiled. He rubbed the stubble on his jaw. He needed a shave and he needed one bad. He looked at Bootjack. The big cowboy had black whiskers and his eyes were bloodshot from lack of sleep. While Jim had shaved in the creek Bootjack napped on the shore. Jim stood in the water in his birthday suit and bathed and shaved. He felt much better when he dressed.

His face had lost most of its marks that had been put upon it by the fists of Big Ike Outland, down there in the clerk's office. His eye was still black, though; took a long time for a black eye to heal. He pushed his boot toe into his partner's ribs.

"Take a shave an' a bath, friend. Both are free."

"About the only thing free in this country."

"We still got free air."

"Some smart boy will figure out some way to charge us for the air we breathe. I wonder how Vivie is?"

"I been thinkin' of her myself."

So the big man had bathed and shaved and Jim had caught a few minutes of much needed sleep. Their horses grazed back in the brush on the long bluejoint grass that was a native to this high Montana range. Their broncs were tired for the distance had been long and they rested for an hour before pushing on toward the big sandstone rock.

"Sure don't see no tracks around here," Bootjack said, searching the ground. "Not a track of a man."

Jim looked at the soil. The wind had whipped away the loose dust and had lain barren the hard soil. There was gravel on the ground, too; he knew that this would not show tracks at any time.

"Well, we'll leave the salt, and ride back into the hills and wait. We can't do no more than that right now 'cause it'll soon be dark."

They went back into the higher country and lit a fire in a canyon and warmed some beans they had stolen from the line-camp. Jim was restless and he carried his rifle to a high ridge, for it was his turn at guard. The dusk was just getting thick when he saw a rider coming in from Larb City. His glasses showed the man to be none other than Rolf Palmer.

Palmer was astraddle a gray horse and he was about three miles away. Jim did not ride out and meet the man; they had no business to settle—they had settled their troubles with six-shooters in Larb City. Jim remembered the blind, terrible jealousy Palmer had shown when Vivie, for some reason only known to a female, had tried to make him "her man." Palmer sure was stuck on Vivie.

He figured that Palmer had found out that Vivie was in bed in Beaver Tail, and he was going into town to see her. But he was surprised to see Palmer turn off the road that led to Beaver Tail and go into the hills. Jim figured the man would pass through a coulee about a mile away. For a moment he had a sneaking fear: had Palmer spotted their camp and was he sneaking in on them?

But that plan was short-lived. Palmer was riding in the open—he was not sneaking through the brush. Nevertheless Jim was in the brush when Palmer rode by. He passed within fifty feet of Jim.

Palmer still had his left arm in a sling, a grim memento of Jim's bullet. He rode down the coulee and disappeared in the ground in the general direction of the O

Bar O Connected spread. Jim gave this thought and realized that the man *had* to be heading for the Outland outfit.

Now why did Palmer ride over to see Big Ike?

Jim rode back to camp. At midnight Bootjack came out and relieved him. Jim did not go back down to the camp in the coulee. He told Bootjack about seeing Palmer heading for the O Bar O Connected and then he went back in the rocks, out of the wind, and he slept there. He slept the way a wild animal sleeps—coiled for warmth, out of the wind. When morning came he was stiff and sore and he rubbed his jaw and said, "Cripes, Bootjack, whiskers again! Don't them things ever get discouraged?"

"An' I used to scrape the down off'n my face, prayin' that it'd soon turn to whiskers. Jim, Palmer an' two men headed back this mornin', goin' for Larb City. Went through about daybreak."

"Who was the two men with him?"

"Big Ike Outlan' an' Toad Graham."

Jim chewed a dried biscuit that had

been in a bin down at the line-camp. "Well, somethin's in the wind, 'cause all the thieves are in Larb City now, I reckon."

"Yeah, but Palmer turned off, an' he done headed for Beaver Tail town, it done looked to this boy."

"Vivie," Jim reminded. "He's wild about her. I wish I hadn't had to shoot Palmer. He seems kinda like a nice fella. But I had that plan of workin' in with that Larb City gang an' findin' out what become of Rusty an' our cattle. An' Palmer pushed me so hard I had to defend myself."

"Never met the gent," Bootjack commented.

They broke camp, which was a simple process, and they headed back into the higher reaches, intending to watch the sandstone rock through fieldglasses. Had the Wild Man been watching them he would have figured they were leaving the country. And Jim was pretty sure that the Wild Man was watching them from some hidden crevice back in the hills.

"He'll prob'ly be suspicious," Jim said. "Up to now the salt has been took here by one man, an' now two ride up."

"That might be right. Look, Jim, we're playin' a wild hand, son; maybe we aren't after the right cards. Mebbeso this Wild Man ain't Pancho, like we figures. We ain't got no proof."

"It's our only chance."

Bootjack thumbed his bottom lip and put his forehead into grooved thought. "Might be, at that. If'n he's Pancho he'll know what become of the herd. Seems to me he's hidin' because somebody's out to kill him."

"That's reasonable."

They got on a windswept high ridge and settled behind a bony backbone of igneous outcropping that ran the length of the hogback. The rocks cut the wind slightly but it was still chilly.

They watched that entire day. Nobody came to get the salt on the rock. The fieldglasses showed the range and its depressions and swells, but no rider—or man on foot—came to the rock.

Jim said, "Wonder if the salt is still there?"

"Nobody's been up to that rock. We've watched close."

"Might've blown it away, even though we did have it in a sack an' we did weigh the sack down with rocks."

"I'll stay here."

Jim rode down slope and reached the rock. To his surprise the salt sack was gone. The rocks they had used to hold it down were still on top of the sandstone. He thought at first that maybe the wind had blown the sack down. But then he realized the wind was not that strong. He looked on the ground but saw no spilt salt nor did he find the sack. But he did find something else.

He found a man's footprint.

And that man had been barefooted.

Jim leaned forward in his saddle and studied the print. But it told him nothing —just the track left by a barefooted man. This was uncanny; he pushed back his hat; he was surprised and this registered on his thin face. They had watched this rock closely; watched it each second—still, the Wild Man had come in and he had taken the salt. He had taken it right from in front of their noses, so to say; and they had not seen him.

Man, we've sure got sharp eyes, eh?, Jim thought.

So great was his surprise that he dismounted and looked again to make sure it really was the track of a barefooted man. He followed the track until it reached the rimrock and there he found the tracks of a horse, down in the coulee. The Wild Man had ridden down the coulee, thereby remaining hidden, and then he had sneaked up over the ledge, had got the sack of salt, and then had ducked back into security again.

Jim followed the hoof-marks until he lost them on a lava bed within half a mile. He cut a circle and came back to Bootjack and he told the man what he knew. Bootjack whistled in surprise and spat.

"Thet gent must be ol' Pancho. He was like a cat, remember. Wisht he could see us 'cause if it is Pancho an' if he saw us he'd ride up to us."

"Lots of *ifs*, Bootjack."

"Maybe we can set out some other bait. We got some ol' biscuits we picked up back at thet line-camp."

Jim smiled. "He's got what he wants, an' he wanted salt. With salt a man can live here 'cause there's lots of game, not to mention O Bar O Connected cows. No, I don't reckon he'd want any biscuits."

"Wish he'd see us closer."

Jim said, "He doesn't expect us up in this country. What gets me is this: Who is he? If he is Pancho Torres, then somethin' sure as heck has happened to Rusty, or Rusty'd be with him. Maybe we're jes' barkin' up the wrong tree again, eh?"

"Could be."

"But we gotta be sure."

They discussed the situation to greater lengths. If somebody had highjacked the U U herd and killed Rusty then Pancho Torres—if this Wild Man was Pancho—must have made his escape. That was one premise. Another was that this was not

Pancho. If it were not the old Mexican then there was only the clue of the red-headed bandit and the buckskin horse.

"We trail this gent," Jim said.

They decided to split up. They would meet the next night at the sandstone rock. Both figured he could do more if he travelled alone, because then a man could remain hidden easier—it is easier to see two men than it is to see one. Both would work the range to the west, for the tracks had gone that way.

Bootjack said, smilingly, "Good luck, Jim."

Jim wished his partner the same. "We'll need it." he said.

18

JIM did not hide himself in the brush. He rode openly through the hills, moving back and forth, for he knew he could not outstalk the Wild Man, whoever he was. The experience with the salt had told him that.

Therefore he did not ride through brush or seek shelter and try to sneak from one point to another. If the Wild Man were Pancho, and if Pancho could get close enough to see him, then the Mexican would surely recognize him. Jim kept going toward the higher lifts of the rough country. He had reasoned that the Wild Man would get as high as he could, for from what Eli Jones had said the Wild Man was a hunted man, and he was hunted by the O Bar O Connected men, Toad Graham and Big Ike Outland. This information posed another riddle. Why did the two O Bar O Connected men hunt for the Wild Man?

To kill him because he lived off rustled O Bar O Connected beef? Or to kill him because of some other reason? Or to kill him in self defense? But why would the Wild Man want to kill Big Ike or Toad Graham?

The whole setup, he decided, was a riddle.

Occasionally he saw Bootjack in the distance, but when afternoon came the big cowhand was out of sight, evidently working the southern section of the rough country. The contour of the land changed rapidly as Jim rode south. The canyons turned into deeper ravines and these in turn became the badlands that were on the north side of the Missouri river. These badlands were gaudy with color—the scarlet and orange and blue and darkness of igneous veins of rock. Here had come the Sioux and the Gros Ventres and the Blackfoot and the Crow for the scarlet and blue and orange pigments to make their terrible war paints. Here they had waged war over these badlands, and occasionally Jim saw graves. These were hung in the gaunt cottonwood trees, platforms made of twigs and leaves and hung by buckskin; these held the skeletons of the warriors killed in combat. From some still came the stench of decay, for these wars were not of the long, long past. There had been fighting last year—last fall, in fact—over these badlands.

But these hanging graves did not interest Jim Carlin. The reds were on reservations, penned in by the army and by hunger—the buffalo was almost gone and the buffalo had fed the redskins on his warpaths. Jim was looking for the Wild Man. But when dusk changed to darkness, he had found no trace of this individual. Once he had seen two O Bar O Connected cowboys riding in the far distance, and he had holed up and watched them come closer; his fieldglasses had let him read the brands on their broncs. The cowhands were miles from the home camp. This was a big outfit and it claimed thousands of acres.

But he had not a whit of interest either in these riders; he just wanted nothing to do with them; he figured they wanted nothing to do with him, either. They were cowhands earning their forty per and found and they evidently wanted no trouble, any more than he wanted trouble with them. He watched them tail a cow out of a bog hole and then they drifted toward the east and moved into two pinpoints that finally fell out of sight. Only then did he ride out of the brush that had hidden him and his bronc.

This was wilderness supreme, the home of the mule-tail deer and the bobcat; occasionally a cougar came down from the Little Rockies during a hard winter; he hunted on the lower reaches and his fangs and claws made inroads into the deer population. Coyotes moved on the edges of his vision, for they were canny and wise and they kept out of rifle range—they were the scavengers and the wisemen on this grass. Once bear had ranged here, but they had moved back into deeper timber, driven there by the rifles of the cowboys, who shot them to protect their calves and cows.

Jim held his bronc on a ridge. From here he could see far to the north, and far across the Canadian Line, some seventy miles away, he saw the uncertain outlines of the Wood Mountain hills. He also saw the bluffs north of Milk River and, for a moment, the loneliness, the beauty, of this land touched him. It came and put away hate and rancor, and he found himself remembering how the sunlight had touched the golden tint of Janet Albers' golden hair.

She was angry with him, now.

But sometimes a woman's anger is short of life, and Jim Carlin hoped this was one of those times. His thoughts swung to his Hell Creek chore of building a homestead. He liked this range and he aimed to stay on his homestead, after this was over. And he wanted Janet there with him.

He thought, *That'll come later*.

He spent the night in the high rimrock overlooking a lonely little valley that was only a mile or so in width. There in the boulders he built a small fire. He warmed some beans and ate some hard biscuits and wondered if he would ever eat a good meal again. Yes, or sleep on a mattress or strawtick. All these things seemed remote and far behind.

He rolled in his blankets but the night, at this higher altitude, was chilly and stubborn. Once he came out of a thin sleep with a jerk and he thought, something was moving out there in the dark. By this time the fire had died and he had no light; only hot ashes glowed weakly.

He listened, braced on one elbow.

But, if man or beast had watched him, that man—or that beast—had left with no further or betraying sound. But there was no more sleep for him. He feigned sleep, lying on the ground; his eyes, though, were wide open. Dawn came and brought a cold, metallic light that lay across this weird, lonesome country. He came out of his blankets, rolled them, restored them to their spot behind his saddle's cantle, tied by the rear strings to the skirt of his kak. He chewed the last of his hard biscuits and secretly cursed an unknown cowboy-cook because he had put too much salt in them. He rode down and drank at a waterhole, the edges of which were encrusted with white alkali. The water tasted as bad as it looked; it was brackish with alkali, but animals had come down to drink; it was the only water hole in miles. He saw the tracks of deer and cattle and wild horses; a coyote had lapped here, too; there were the wider paw marks of a prairie wolf.

He drank very sparingly. This alkali water raised heck with a man's guts. Besides having alkali, it had gypsum, too. His horse refused to drink, expecting there would be better water somewhere ahead. He was right, too. About ten miles further, toward noon, the animal scented water; he led the way to a small spring that sent a tiny rivulet of water out of a rock. Jim scooped out the muddy soil and made a basin. It took the water an hour to become deep enough so his horse could drink. Even at that the drink was short.

But he found the footprints of a barefooted man in the soft earth. He went to one knee and judged them very fresh. He stood up and looked at the brush around him. He cupped his hands and hollered, "Pancho, oh, Pancho! Pancho Torres, this is Jim Carlin. Do you hear me, friend. *Amigo mio*, you hear Jim Carlin?"

Only the echo of his voice from the steep slant of the hill.

Again he looked at the track. He tried to make a mental comparison between this track and the one he had discovered around the rock on which he and Bootjack James had placed the salt. But this was impossible. All barefoot men left about the same track. But he did not think there were *two* barefooted men in this wilderness of brush and rock.

The Wild Man was trailing him. He had not drunk of the alkali spring; he had known about this sweet-water spring, and he had filled his belly here. And it had been just a short while before.

"Pancho, you hear me, Jim Carlin?"

The brush sounded behind him; he

pivoted, nerves tight. But the man who stood there was only Bootjack James. His partner's big, bewhiskered face was good to see, but the man's voice was almost a whisper.

"He's back in the brush, Jim. He trailed you. I saw you both from the ridge."

"You recognize him?"

"Too much beard on him, 'though my fieldglasses picked him out good."

"Can't be Pancho. If it was him he'd come when I called."

"Didn't look like him to me. He walked bent over a lot, an' Pancho was purty straight, although he was an ol' button."

Jim said, "Swing out."

Bootjack went back into the buck-brush. Rifle in hand, Jim walked ahead; he left his bronc in the clearing. He went about fifty yards, the brush high around him; suddenly, his arms were pinned to his sides. The attack was noiseless; the man rushed on him; Jim never knew of him until two steel bands were around his arms. The man was behind him, clamping down; his head was hard against Jim's spine.

"Drop rifle."

Jim realized his rifle would do him no good. He could not use it. He heard it fall to the ground.

He could not see the man's face, for the man's face was down. He looked over his shoulder, twisting his neck; he could see the man's back and rump. The man was almost naked except for a tattered pair of pants. He had no shirt; his skin was bare; the skin clung like parchment to a bony, skinny torso. The man was old.

"Pancho?"

"Pancho? I no *sabe*?"

The voice sounded strained. But Jim's heart jumped at the word *sabe*. A Spanish word and nobody on this far northern range could speak Mexican except a Mexican. Jim did not struggle. He was afraid the man had a knife. He could easily have a knife in a scabbard at the front part of his belt—the hidden part.

"Pancho, *Yo soy* Jim Carlin." He put it in English. "Pancho, I'm Jim Carlin."

"*Tu conoco me?*" You know me.

"Si, Pancho." Jim talked rapidly in Border Mexican. He thought he felt the arms relax.

Let those arms relax a trifle more, and he'd make his play—knife or no knife. He'd go down at the knees and twist, his fists rising to hit the man in the guts.

He never got the chance.

Suddenly the man was jerked backwards. His grip was so hard that he pulled Jim down to the earth with him. Jim caught a glimpse of Bootjack James and he knew Bootjack had jumped the man from behind.

He also saw the man's face. A pinched, dirty face, thick with a beard touched with iron-gray, and he hit the ground. The impact broke the man's iron grip. Then Jim was on his feet and Bootjack was sitting on the Wild Man, holding him to the earth. Bootjack had his massive hands on the man's shoulders, his big weight was pinning the man's middle.

Despite this, though, the Wild Man almost got loose. Finally Bootjack held him and the man was limp. Only his eyes moved and they were darting, swift things —they touched Bootjack, they flicked to Jim. They were blank and stupid and yet they were bright with the wariness of a hunted animal.

Jim looked at Bootjack, who looked up at him. The big man's eyes were thick with something that was akin to sorrow. Then they both looked at the feverish, wasted face of the Wild Man.

Jim said, "Pancho Torres, sure as heck."

Bootjack said, "An' his mind is sick, Jim; he don't know us."

Jim squatted. "I'll try some Mex." He talked rapidly but the eyes were blank as they watched him. The dirty, sun-cracked lips did not move. Jim kept on talking. He mentioned Rusty and he talked of little incidents that had occurred in Texas.

It seemed to him the eyes cleared. Suddenly the cracked lips said. "Jim, *muchacho mio*, Jim Carlin. You are a ghost, no?"

Jim was sitting crosslegged then; he held the battered, ugly head of the old man against his thighs; he stroked the matted, wiry hair. There was something in his eyes that wasn't pain or surprise. It was the slow look of a man who had at last found an old friend.

"Let him go, Bootjack."

Bootjack stood up.

Pancho Torres looked up at Jim. "Jim, and Bootjack. I guess—my mind—it isn't right. They hunt me—men hunt me—Texas?"

"We came for you and Rusty. We came out of Texas."

"No believe."

"Feel my face."

The claw went upward, the nails sunken and worn; it was sandpaper running across Jim's face. The claw went down.

"You let me up, no?"

"Bootjack isn't on you."

"Oh, *si*." A smile now—a timid,

boyish smile strangely out of place against the seamed, bearded face. "You come for me, Jim?"

"And Rusty, too."

The head shook slowly. "Rusty, poor Rusty." And Pancho lowered his head into his hands and sobbed. Then his sobbing turned into wild tears. Jim held him on one side; Bootjack's immense hands held him on the other.

Jim's eyes met that of his partner.

Both were silent while the old Mexican wept.

19

THEY worked the rest of that day and most of the next before they got a full measure of sanity into the warped, twisted brain of Pancho Torres, the Mexican. At times Jim was on the edge of utter despair, fearing that the memory of the old man was lost forever. This fear was also apparent in the broad face of Bootjack James.

But they kept asking questions, they repeated and repeated, and they brought back memories of Texas, of certain horses on the old U U outfit; they talked about Jim's mother and dad. Some times a bit of sanity would come, and then it would be gone; and the eyes of the old man would be dead and without color. They would be only deep coals set under the ledges of his craggy brows.

Jim searched the man's head for signs of a blow or a scar that might have indicated some calamity had fallen on Pancho, but he found not a trace of a scar. The man had lived a hunted, persecuted life; this had in turn broken his brain. Jim stood up and looked at Bootjack.

"Maybe we come too late?"

"We have to keep trying, Jim."

That night they took turns standing guard for they did not want Pancho Torres to sneak away into the night. When Jim slept he slept beside his old friend and in the night Pancho's gnarled hand found his and the old man murmured, "Jimmer, Jimmer. Jimmer, my boy, my boy." This was the first time he had called Jim by the old nickname only he alone had used. And Jim had sat up and he had said, "Pancho, talk to Jimmer."

Only silence.

But the Mexican did not try to escape. He slept like the proverbial log. When morning came they shared the last of their rations with him. Bootjack shot a cotton-tail rabbit; they skinned it; they cooked it over the fire. Jim and his partner decided to take Pancho into town for medical attention. They did not let him know their plan; he would have objected, and he might have tried to escape.

"But the doc don't tend to us nesters," Bootjack said.

"Pancho ain't no nester."

"But you an' me is. He wouldn't look at you when you got done tanglin' with Big Ike Outland."

Pancho looked up. "Big Ike Outland . . ." He repeated the words about three times. He sat with his back against a boulder. He quit speaking and he looked at his bare feet. He had a childish interest in his bare feet.

Jim repeated, "Big Ike Outland," and watched the man.

No response.

They saddled their broncs. Pancho would ride with Jim for the first half of the distance, riding in his saddle with Jim behind him. That way Jim could keep his arms around the old man.

Bootjack said, "We're ready to bust camp."

Pancho said, "Wait a minute, men."

The sanity, the clarity, of his voice made Jim wheel, and he dropped the reins of his horse to the ground.

Jim asked, "Pancho, what do you say?"

Pancho looked at him and Jim noticed the man's eyes were no longer clouded and dirty, they were clear and clean. Pancho did not get to his feet. He remained sitting with his back against the rock.

"It comes back to me now, men."

Jim looked at Bootjack, whose mouth hung open. He went over and sat beside Pancho. Bootjack hunkered on the other side of the recluse.

And Pancho, speaking clearly, told his story. And as Jim listened the color went out of him, the life of him became weak, and his heart pounded with a great dislike for each word the old man said.

But each word, he knew, was true. For Pancho Torres said those words.

Each word clarified many doubts.

They had crossed the Missouri River, Pancho and Rusty, and the wildness, the hell, in Rusty had come out in full, dirty blossom. Rusty had met Big Ike Outland and Toad Graham and the deal had been made.

"Rusty, he double-cross you—he sell herd. Sell whole herd, he does."

"Where?" Jim asked quietly.

"Over that way." The claw made a sweeping motion toward the east. "Block Hills, U U cows go. Gold there. Rusty sell them all, keep money."

Jim's eyes met those of Bootjack. The big man's eyes showed his mental suffering. Jim wondered, idly, just what his own eyes looked like. He hoped they didn't hold the bleak hell that showed in the gaze of Bootjack James.

"Double crossed us, Jim."

Jim said, "My only brother."

"No wonder we couldn't find a trace of the U U iron on them O Bar O Connected cows we killed."

"Where is Rusty now?" Jim wanted to know.

Pancho Torres shook his head. "I theenk he ees dead, men. I theenk Big

Ike an' Toad Graham they keel heem for hees money."

Jim stood up. Now he knew why Pancho Torres, the peaceful, joking Mexican, had become the Wild Man, and he knew why the two O Bar O Connected men had tried to kill him. Pancho had been out to gun them because he had thought they had killed Rusty. And they had been riding with rifles to kill Pancho to silence him.

"Rusty ain't dead." Jim said.

Pancho stared. "Why you say that?"

Jim told about the two bandits who had robbed the county clerk's office. "One of them was a redhead, an' he rode that Sonny hoss critter. I'd know that bronc anywhere: thet hoss was Sonny. Later on a redheaded gent an' a pard robbed the bank over to Custer Bend."

"Maybe he not Rusty?"

"There's a chance of that being true." Jim was silent for a long moment. "I hope it is true."

"They keel Rusty. That's why I try to

keel them. They keel heem an' rob heem."

"You see his grave?"

"No . . ."

Jim looked at Bootjack. "My theory was right when I headed for Larb City. We'll find Rusty there if he's alive. Well, the kid sure hung the ol' doublecross onto us, eh?"

"We lost the whul herd." Bootjack said mournfully. "But the herd don't amount to anythin', compared with Rusty. If they killed they've got to pay to me, even if Rusty did sink so low as to doublecross us."

"My words, too."

Pancho Torres was moaning. He lay on the wind-packed soil and moaned like a sick, beaten puppy. Jim watched him and pity was a strong force in him. Rusty had always been wild and he had been the favorite of his father and mother because he was the younger. Jim did not like to admit it but he laid this at the foot of his dead mother. She had spoiled Rusty.

But those thoughts, scattered as they

were, had no import here. Rusty had sold the herd and Pancho claimed Rusty had been killed by the O Bar O Connected outfit.

But there was more than one red-headed man in the world, he finally admitted. But that bronc had been Sonny.

Bootjack asked, "What's next, Jim?"

"Big Ike Outland," Jim said. "Yes, and Toad Graham, too."

"They're in Larb City. They went there with Rolf Palmer."

"They might have headed back for their spread."

Bootjack shook his head. "Would have had to be in the night. Otherwise we'd've seen them. But we could check first at the O Bar O Connected."

Jim said, "Okay, but we'd best get Pancho to town first."

They rode for two hours and they were in a brush-filled coulee, following an old trail ground out by buffalo going down into the valley for water, when the two riders topped the ridge. Sheriff Mike Albers held his right hand high in the

Sioux sign of peace and came down the slope, shale sliding ahead of his bronc.

Jim and Bootjack reined in, hands on their guns. Pancho Torres started whimpering, then suddenly he stopped; he stared toward the sheriff.

Behind the sheriff rode Rolf Palmer.

"He's got a warrant for us," Bootjack murmured. "It means jail if we go with him."

Jim felt very tired. "We know what happened to the herd now. We could tell the sheriff what Pancho knows and from then on he'd have to act or get out of office. And we have to get Pancho to town."

"What'll we do?"

"Just sit here an' wait for what comes."

So they sat their broncs and the pair rode up. Sheriff Albers peered at Pancho and then looked at Jim, a question in his eyes. Jim told him who Pancho was and he told him the information Pancho had given them. Sheriff Albers looked at Rolf Palmer and Palmer nodded.

"Jes' the way we figerred it out, sheriff," Palmer said.

Jim asked, "You figured what out?"

Sheriff Mike Albers answered the question. Jim had Palmer gauged wrongly. Palmer was an undercover man for the territorial government. He had been sent out to track down the Larb City gang.

Jim asked, "Then why did you jump me?"

Palmer answered that. "I never thought it would go as far as guns, Jim. I made an error there; I pushed you too hard. I wanted to work in better with the Big Boss and I figured that if I pistol-whipped you and ran you out of Larb City it would be an *in* for me."

"I could've killed you."

Palmer nodded. "It was all my mistake. Then when Vivie played up to you it drove me wild." He shook his head slowly. "Jim, I say it here, honestly and openly: I love Vivie. I'm wild about her. Maybe that seems an odd statement, coming from a detective, especially when she's a dance hall girl, but it's the God honest truth. I want to marry her."

The man was very sincere. Jim felt the edge of this sincerity and did not doubt it for a moment. Vivie had made a mistake back there along her days, but that mistake was not too serious. Many a big rancher in this section had as his wife an ex-dancehall girl and most of them made good wives.

Jim asked, "How is Vivie?"

Vivie was getting better. She and Janet had spent much time together. Janet had her in the sheriff's home to take care of her.

"Janet still mad at me?" Jim asked the sheriff.

The sheriff smiled. "Sure, she's mad, an' she tol' me why—you stole her badge an' her gun. But I kinda think she'll get over it. You two sure haven't known each other very long but she sure is excited about you, Carlin."

"Hope she stays that way."

"I figure she will."

Jim leaned back, his arms around

Pancho. The world looked a lot better. He had his old friend back, evidently the sheriff was dropping charges against him, and although he and Bootjack had lost their herd, they still had the homestead on Hell Creek. A man can rebuild when he's as young as they were.

"Palmer," Jim said, "I want your hand, sir."

"With pleasure, Jim."

They shook hands. Jim said, "No hard feelings."

Palmer said, "I'd cotton to have you stand up with me an' Vivie, Carlin."

"With pleasure, sir."

Bootjack cut in with, "Where you men headin' for, an' why?"

For a moment there was silence. Then a magpie down the draw took up his raucous call. This sound died. Jim looked from the sheriff to Rolf Palmer, and then back to Sheriff Mike Albers.

Finally Albers said slowly, "We got a posse over the hill. There's no whiskey in this bunch. We got all the evidence we need. I've held back because of lack of evidence. Palmer has evidence now. The redhead and the other bandits are all in Larb City."

"So is Outland an' Graham," Jim said.

Sheriff Albers nodded. "The O Bar O Connected furnished broncs for the bandits. For some time that spread has been workin' in with these train holdups and bank robberies. We got the whole bunch in Larb City."

"Then what?" Jim asked.

"We're ridin' to clean them out," the sheriff said quietly. Bootjack glanced at Jim.

Jim said, "We ride with you, men."

20

THE sheriff agreed to permit one of the posse's members to ride into town with Pancho Torres but the old Mexican would not stand for it. He put up the argument that the O Bar O Connected outfit had tried to kill him, had tried to hunt him down like a predatory animal, and he would not go to Beaver Tail and leave Jim and Bootjack. So the sheriff had looked inquiringly at Jim.

Jim said, "If I was in his boots, I'd say the same words."

"He don't wear boots," Bootjack said.

There was a hasty, nervous laugh from the posse.

"Let 'em ride along," the sheriff said gruffly.

Pancho rode alone now, astraddle a horse that had been led by one of the posse's men, who had taken an extra bronc along. Jim found himself riding beside Rolf Palmer. It was almost ironical that he and Palmer ride side by side. Jim remembered his bullet sending the detective into the dust there on Larb City's main drag.

"Did you aim to kill me, Palmer?"

Rolf Palmer showed a small smile. "I figured you was real slow with a gun, bein' only a cowpoke, an' not a gunslinger. I figured I'd be so far ahead of you thet I could just hold a gun on you an' laugh you outa town. 'Stead of that, you outdrew me. I'll never pull that stunt again, believe you me."

"Were you the gent that let me an' Vivie out of the sod shack?"

"How did you guess it?"

"Caught a good glimpse of you in the night. Heard your voice, too. Sure didn't seem logical, an' I figured until now I was wrong. You sure did me a good turn."

"I wanted to help you an' Vivie."

"I want to thank you."

They rode in silence then, not a word between them, and the sounds consisted of the creak of leather, the plod of hoofs. Dust was fine and sweet in a man's nostrils, and the wind talked quietly through the sagebrush.

Jim said, "I've done tol' you about my brother Rusty an' our herd. I feel sure that was Rusty that held up the clerk;, I know the horse was Sonny. Did you ever see that redhead in Larb City, Palmer?"

"No, I didn't."

"Did you hear anythin' about him?"

Palmer had heard talk about the redhead. But the redhead seemed to be a very mysterious figure. Only one man—Fox Turner—seemed to have anything to do with the redhead. Turner had been with the redhead on the hold-up of the county clerk. He had also ridden with the redhead when the Custer Bend bank had been looted.

"I remember him," Jim said. "I saw him in the Pine Tree Saloon. You sure he was the gent thet rode with the redhead?"

"I know he was."

"Who is the Big Boss?"

Palmer shrugged his good shoulder.

"You got me stumped there, Carlin. I got a hunch he's nobody else than Big Ike Outland."

Jim considered that. He remembered how the speaking tube had distorted the Big Boss' voice. Jim didn't feel very good. This had been a day of sweeping revelations; and those revelations had not been cheerful. The U U herd was gone. Pancho's words had cinched down his suspicions that Rusty had doublecrossed him and Bootjack. He had no hate toward his brother. Instead he had pity. Even though he and Rusty had never been too close, Rusty was still his own flesh and blood. And a man cannot hate his brother.

He found himself hoping that Rusty was dead. Or if he were not dead, then he hoped he would not be in Larb City. This posse meant business. They were bound to wipe out a longrider hangout. They were not all townsmen from Beaver Tail. Some were territorial hands sent out from the capitol in Helena. They were fighters and they were tough; they toted law-stars under their shirts.

Jim glanced at Sheriff Mike Albers. Up until now he had figured the sheriff was a sort of an easy-going gent, easily fooled. But all hesitation, all uncertainty, seemed to abandon the lawman, pushed out by the urgency of the moment. Albers was all business now.

The sheriff held up his hand and the posse members surrounded him. Albers spoke in an unhurrried voice.

They were about twelve miles from Larb City. He figured that the outlaws would have guards stationed. He did not want those guards to see his posse. Therefore he was sending out scouts to reconnoiter.

Palmer said, "Count me as one, sheriff."

"All right, Rolf."

Jim noticed that he and Bootjack, although both now knew the terrain of this section, were not selected. The sheriff's logic was apparent. Jim's brother was one of the longrider legion. The sheriff did not entirely trust either Jim or his partner. Therefore the U U men stayed in camp.

They made camp in a draw, out of sight from any possible scouts for the Larb City bunch. They were not allowed to light a fire so they ate cold chuck packed by the women of Beaver Tail. Jim noticed that old Pancho literally tore into his food, and he knew that the old man was starving. From here on out it would be the easy life for Pancho, doing chores on the Hell Creek homestead.

Sheriff Albers did not ride with his scouts. He paced back and forth, back and forth. The rest of the posse members either played cards or talked in low voices; occasionally you could hear a rifle-breech snap shut, or hear the click of a .45's loading gate going into position. There was very little conversation, Jim noticed. What there was was short and had no serious meaning. Jokes, mostly. Jim lay on his side and dozed; Bootjack sat over against the cut; Pancho Torres sat beside Jim. Finally, toward late afternoon, scouts came drifting back into camp. They were furtive men, and they came out of the brush without warning.

"They're all in town, men."

"Where's Rolf Palmer?"

Palmer had ridden openly into Larb City. He should have been back by now. Palmer did not show up and minutes stretched out and the dusk became a thick blanket. Maybe something had happened to Palmer?

Had the bandits got wise—had Rolf Palmer ridden into a trap—had—?

Palmer came out of the buckbrush.

"They're all in town," the man said brusquely. "It's time to hit, men. Sheriff, outline your plan of attack."

The sheriff wasted no words. They would encircle Larb City and then, at a called signal, they would move in on foot, leaving their horses back in coulees and behind boulders.

"That signal will be what?" Jim wanted to know.

"The word *Beaver Tail*."

Jim nodded.

Men looked at each other.

They rode out, moving through the twilight; a horse stumbled over a rock, his rider laughed and jerked him upright. Jim noticed that the laugh had been too shrill. He rode close to Palmer.

"See any sign of my redheaded brother?"

Palmer shook his head.

"The Big Boss in town?"

"So I heard. Up in his office, I guess. They say he has a tunnel that leads upstairs through a secret stairway. I don't see how it is possible that he keeps his identity hidden all the time."

"He must have it worked out," Jim had to admit.

Jim had a number of thoughts. Yes, the Big Boss sure was an elusive figure, and Rusty—if the redhead was really Rusty—was a pretty elusive gent, too. It did not seem logical that the redhead was Rusty. When he, Jim, was in Larb City, Rusty, had he been in the outlaw town, would surely have looked him up. Or would he have contacted him? Rusty had the sign of the doublecross burned into his soul. Maybe he had not dared.

No matter which way Jim viewed the situation, no matter what angle it drew consideration, the problem was an unhealthy one, making him a little sick at the pit of his belly.

Sheriff Albers said, "This is it, men. They had added two unwilling members of the Larb City bunch to their numbers. These two were guards that the advance members of the posse had slugged into sleep, before making prisoners of them. Now they had them trussed and ready for questioning.

But the sheriff did not question them.

"Scatter out, men, an' go ahead on foot. We got a serious chore ahead of us an' some of us might get shot. We gotta admit that fact. If you get wounded, and you can't get back to this spot, then lie down and wait until one of us finds you. Don't waste valuable energy tryin' to crawl back here."

Jim listened. He looked at Bootjack. Bootjack was looking at the ground. Jim looked at old Pancho Torres. The old man's bony hands gripped his rifle and his seamed face was savage with thoughts only he would ever understand.

"We got the doc here, as you all know. Doc, you stay back here, and wait, eh?"

"I'll do that, Mike."

Jim said, "You'd patch me up, wouldn't you, Doc? Even if I am a damned nester, as you once called me."

Jim was serious.

The medico said, "Fella, don't rub me. I was wrong. I'll admit that now. When I said that I didn't know what skunks this Big Ike an' Toad Graham were. Is that enough?"

"Enough," Jim said.

The sheriff smiled and outlined their attack. He would give them fifteen minutes to surround the town.

"At the end of that time we hit in, men. I'll be over in the rocks to the south side of Larb City an' I'll give the *Beaver Tail* war-cry. Keep movin' in then, an' keep rememberin' the call word. I don't crave to have one of you shoot another member of my posse."

Jim said, "A second by-word would come in handy, if them bandits got onto the first one, sheriff."

"Good idea Jim. *Milk River.*"

The word ran through the men. The second call-word: Milk River, Milk River, Milk River.

The sheriff said, "Jim, you're on my right. Bootjack, on my left. Pancho, you go with Palmer."

Pancho Torres showed dirty, crooked teeth. "*Con mucho gusto*," he said.

21

JIM spoke to Bootjack. "If we run into Rusty I can't cross guns with him."

"Neither can I, Jim."

Jim said, "But mebbe we won't run into him. Mebbe this redheaded bandit is some other gent, even if he does set astraddle Sonny horse. Meebe Rusty is dead an' buried."

"Be far better, Jim."

Sheriff Mike Albers had, of course, heard their conversation. But if it had any effect on him he did not show it.

"Come on, men."

They had waited their allotted length of time, and so they moved ahead. But first Jim looked at Bootjack and Jim murmured, "Good luck, my friend."

Bootjack murmured something and Jim realized that he was pretty tense.

The dusk was thick, lying close to the ground. By this time perhaps the denizens of Larb City had possibly discovered that their two guards were gone. Had this discovery been made the town would possibly be ready for the posse. And the *whang* of a rifle bullet against a nearby boulder told Jim the discovery had been made.

"Damn it," the sheriff grunted, "they're wise to us."

Bootjack said, "That bullet sure didn't sound good to me."

"Too danged close." Jim smiled.

Sheriff Mike Albers said, "Spread wider, an' rush for the buildings. We got to get in among them buildings."

Jim said, "Only plan we got," and ran ahead. He ran stooped over, carrying his rifle; it was about fifty yards to the alley. Ahead of him dust lifted as a steel-jacketed rifle bullet hit the earth. This was going to be a tough one, he realized. When this was over a few of the boys wouldn't fill saddles again.

He heard the sheriff yell something, and for a moment he thought the lawman had stopped a lead; a quick glance backward showed him the sheriff was unharmed, but had just given out a warwhoop.

Already the battle was raging across town. Dogs barked, women screamed, and guns made their loud, ugly noises. Jim hit the alley and ducked into a barn. Horses reared against their tie-ropes and a sorrel had reared up and had got both forefeet into the manger. They stared toward Jim, eyes round.

Jim stopped. He said, "Sonny horse, Sonny."

The buckskin was an old hand; he was not worried. He of all the horses was quiet; he stood at his manger; he looked at Jim. Jim went up to him and petted him and felt of his brand. U U iron.

Jim repeated, "Sonny horse," and the full meaning of the buckskin's presence fell on him with a heavy force. Sonny was in Larb City. Sonny was the redhead's top horse. Then, following that logic, the redhead was in town, too.

But that logic, he knew, did not have to be right. The redhead could have ridden a different bronc and might be out of town. You don't ride the same horse all the time, especially when you ride a horse hard away from the scene of a holdup. A horse plays out.

Jim hacked the ropes and turned the broncs loose, including Sonny. The buckskin would not leave the barn, though; the other horses rushed out so fast they jammed in the door, and that side of the barn splintered. They broke out on the alley, running wildly; their hoofs were mad and insistent; they wanted no part of this war put on them by man's greed and killer lust.

"Sonny, get out of here. This barn might catch on fire."

Jim pounded the buckskin on the rump with his rifle barrel, and the horse trotted outside, holding his head to his left so he would not tramp on his trailing hackamore rope.

He stood for a moment inside the barn and he listened to the sounds of battle that were in this badland town. He had a touch of fear for a bullet doesn't care who it kills and the ironical thought that perhaps this outlaw hangout—far back in these gaunt, hungry-looking badlands of Montana—would be the scene of his death was not a bit comforting, either. Then he brushed these thoughts, alarming as they were, away; they fell back before the remembrance that Big Ike Outland and Toad Graham were in Larb City.

And maybe Rusty, too.

He remembered the upstairs of the Pine Tree Saloon, with its cribs and its doors, and he remembered sitting in the barren, duty room up there, listening to the disguised and booming voice of the Big Boss. Palmer figured that the Big Boss was none other than Big Ike Outland, and he had a date to keep with the O Bar O Connected cowman. So he headed for the rear of the Pine Tree.

The distance was not far: not more than a hundred feet. But to get to the back of the Pine Tree he had to cross the alley. He moved along the edge of the barn, watching the back porch of the Pine Tree, and he saw the rifle when it sent out its lead toward him—the rifleman was using black powder and his smoke gave him away. Jim jumped, but he knew, later, the gesture had been foolish; had the bullet hit him it would have smacked into his flesh before he made his sidewise jump. But as he moved he raised his rifle and he sent three fast shots up onto the balcony. The man moved out, coming ahead, and he jackknifed over the bannister, his rifle falling to the alley. Then he slid ahead and landed face down with a sickening thud in the dust.

Jim vaulted up the backstairs, three steps at a time. He expected another rifle to talk, but none raised its voice, and he was on the porch. Here the harpies were prone to sit in the evening, talking about the men of the day and preparing for the men of the night; there were no girls on the balcony, though. He ripped open the door and entered the hall.

The faint, sickening odor of cheap perfume came to him, and with this was mingled the smell of black powder, each blending one to the other, and giving the final odor a smell that was anything but pleasant. A girl looked out from a half open door, not even holding a towel against her, and she said, "Cowboy, how goes the battle, eh?" With the scent of the perfume was now the scent of cheap whiskey.

Evidently she had mistaken him for an outlaw. "We'll win, sister," Jim said.

"I'm ready to make a run for it," she said.

Jim said, "You oughta at least put on your shoes. The alley is full of ol' nails an' broken bottles."

"Why, how sweet of you, cowboy."

The door banged shut.

Jim could hear the other harpies wrangling and hollering, evidently grabbing what few possessions they had preparatory to making a run out of Larb City. He jerked open a door, but it was not the door he wanted; a girl was in the room, arguing with her room mate—these had all their clothes on, ready for the trail.

"We're runnin' for it, cowboy."

"The Big Boss?" Jim grunted. "Where is he?"

"Two doors down."

Jim jerked at the doorknob. The room was silent, nobody moved; he jerked again. He said, "Big Boss, they're rushin' us. We gotta make a run for it, Big Boss. You hear me?"

No answer.

He kicked at the panel and the second time his boot went through. He got a hole big enough for his arm to enter and his arm went in. He found the inside key and turned it and the door opened.

He went into a room that was ornately finished with hardwood furniture. There was a big desk, fine carpets were on the floor, and through it all was the cloyish odor of perfume. But Jim had no interest in the room or its costly furnishings. He was interested only in the man who stood against the far wall.

He never forgot that moment when he and that man stood and looked at each other. To the end of his life he remembered that terrible moment.

Finally his voice said, "Rusty!"

Was it his voice that said that one word: Rusty? It didn't sound like his voice. It sounded like the agonized voice of a man he did not know.

"Jim, eh?"

Rusty's voice was the same. Low and quiet and holding that scheming note. And Rusty's face was the same, too. Thin and weak, with its red whiskers close to the pale skin, with its shifty, weak eyes.

Even Rusty's hands were the same. Long, slender, without callouses, the hands of a man who handled a gun but never handled a rope.

Jim asked, "And you're the Big Boss, eh?"

"I am."

Jim said, and he had his voice now: "You stole my herd, an' you stole Bootjack's share of the herd. You held up the clerk in Beaver Tail and you looked at me with those flat ugly eyes. But you rode Sonny and that gave you away, Mama's Boy."

"Leave our mother out of this!"

Jim looked at the .45 in Rusty's hand. His own gun hung limply from his forefinger. When he looked up his eyes were honest and they held only contempt. There was no fear, no dishonesty, in his eyes. And these elements were in the eyes of his brother.

"You didn't even get to me to talk to me, your soul was too black. I was foolish enough to play into your hands and you talked to me through that big tube to disguise your voice. You made a fool of me."

"I've done that for years."

Jim said, "That's true." For another moment they stood and looked at each other. Outside the sound of men fighting, the report of rifles, the snarl of six-shooters, came into the darkening room, breaking the silence into tiny shreds. *Milk River*, came the call; with it was *Beaver Tail*.

Jim said, "You're losin' your gang.

Outside they're fallin' under the rifles of law-abidin' men. You came up here to pack your filthy money and try to make a break. I can see it in your yellow, dirty eyes."

Rusty shrugged, but his eyes never left his brother.

A great, wonderful loathing entered Jim. He knew now, for sure, that he did not hate his brother; he felt only pity toward him. He realized that his brother had not killed him when he had had a chance; instead, he had locked him in the sod shack, with Vivie. But then memory reminded him that, at the time of their imprisonment, the Big Boss had been out of town, holding up the Custer Bend Bank. Maybe, had they been penned in the sod shack when Rusty had returned, he would have ordered them shot. But it made no difference to Jim, now.

Jim said, "I could kill you, Rusty. I could send a bullet between those narrow eyes of yours. But I won't darling brother, I won't. I'm going to let you live.

I hope you get out of this mess alive, but I doubt if you will."

"That's nice of you, brother." Rusty's voice was ironical.

Jim overlooked the cynicism. "I want you to keep on living. I want you to remember good ol' Bootjack—yes, an' Pancho Torres, too. You had your stooges tryin' to kill Pancho. Yes, I hope you live and this rotten, dirty acid seeps into your soul and eventually kills you."

"Have you had your say?"

"Yes."

"Then get t'hell out."

Jim had his Colt level. He backed toward the door. "I don't trust you," he said. He was very sick at his belly. Maybe it was the stinking odor of the cloyish, feminine perfume; maybe his thoughts had run against his belly nerves. He got to the door and pivoted, and the partition hid him from Rusty. He was again in the hall. And then, coming out of nowhere, the bullet hit him in the high right ribs.

The shock almost doubled him, adding to the pain in his belly. Across the way he glimpsed Big Ike Outland, crouching behind the bannister, gun up for another shot. Between them was the open space and below this was the floor of the saloon. Big Ike had shot across this space.

Jim thought, *my gun is heavy* . . .

Big Ike shot again, but he was too anxious, and his lead went wide. Jim was on one knee now, holding his .45 in both hands, and he found his sights for the moment it required him to shoot.

The Colt kicked, lifted, settled.

His first bullet connected, his second missed. Big Ike never shot again. He grunted something and came to his feet. He tried to raise his hands to his belly, but he couldn't; his .45 dropped and fell to the floor of the saloon.

Jim watched, gun ready. Some of the shock had left him, and in its place was a steadiness.

Big Ike said, very clearly, "By Gawd, you shot me, Carlin!" and he said no more. He bent over the bannister, and he looked as though he were very, very tired. Jim heard the bannister creak under the man's weight, and then the entire section broke from its moorings.

Big Ike fell to the floor of the saloon, and the wreckage fell on top of him. Jim was on his feet, his knees uncertain and weak, and he caught the smell of smoke. Already he could see flame starting across the floor of the saloon. He thought, Rusty'll be trapped, and then he ran, as best he could, to the back veranda. But caution was with him, and before he stepped out, he peered into the alley.

He recognized the two men as posse members and he called, "Jim Carlin, comin' down!" and they pivoted, guns rising to cover the veranda, and he guessed at their nervousness by this unneeded precaution. He started down the steps but his knees gave way and he slid and fell and they caught him.

"Big Ike Outland, we drove him in there, Carlin!"

Jim panted, "I—I—got him."

"You see any sign of the Big Boss?"

Jim found himself shaking his head. He

realized he had lied instinctively. "I looked but couldn't find him."

The other man said, "Lord, listen to the rifle fire out in front."

Jim nodded. He doubled and vomited, and they held him. The sudden flare of gunpowder and lead had told him that Rusty had tried to make his escape out the front way. By this time maybe Rusty was dead. Well, he had had some speck of respect for his brother; he had not tried to break out the back of the saloon. Had he done that he might have forced Jim to shoot at him. Or Jim might have seen him die under the lead of the posse.

Jim said, "The poor, stupid fool.

"What's that, Jim?"

Jim didn't repeat the words; there was no use. They would not understand them, anyway. He felt better but yet he lurched as he went down the alley. The two men hurried to the front of the Pine Tree.

Smoke blew in, hiding the dirtiness of Larb City, and with it came hot ashes, for the wind was rising. Jim saw that the town was doomed. The guns, for the most part, had died; occasionally he heard gunfire, but it was scattered and distant. He wondered, Where is Bootjack?, and then his friend was beside him, holding him.

"Jim, they shot you?"

"My high ribs I'll—I'll live Bootjack. Man it's good to see you, all in one piece."

"Where's Pancho?"

"I don't know."

"They—they killed Rusty. He tried to make his break from the saloon's front door. They shot him—down."

Jim said, "I talked with him."

Bootjack had his arm around him and that arm was solid and strong.

"I don't hate him," Jim said. "He was the Big Boss." Jim tried to keep his voice from trembling.

"So we heard. I'm—sorry for him, Jim; for you, too."

Jim glanced at the big, honest face. He saw the tears in Bootjack's eyes; he realized his eyes held tears, too.

"Maybe he wanted it that way, Bootjack."

Bootjack said, "God bless you, Rusty."

They walked to their horses. Larb City men were being brought in disarmed and with their hands high. Posse men were corralling them preparatory to tying their arms. The confusion had settled down to the ugly job of cleaning-up the town. The fire would destroy the buildings; the flame of it was high. The doc looked at Jim's ribs and said, "Not too bad, not too good. But you can ride. Head for town, and I'll rebandage you there."

Sheriff Albers said, "Head for town, you two. We got enough hands."

Jim asked, "Pancho?"

Albers said, "Here he comes. An' by golly, he's got that Toad Graham ahead of him, he has. Thet ol' hellion done captured him. An' jus' listen to Toad blabber. Pancho, come over here."

"Jimmer, you hurt?"

Jim smiled, "Not much, fella. You comin' with us?"

"*Si, pronto.*"

They rode then toward the cowtown of Beaver Tail, and Pancho sobbed over the death of Rusty, and big Bootjack looked at the Montana horizon and did not see it, and Jim Carlin rode silent as he remembered.

Finally Jim said, "There'll be better days ahead on Hell Crick for the three of us."

Bootjack said, "You mean the four of us, Jim. Little Janet is waitin'—and fear is terrible company."

Jim said, "I'd best ride ahead."

Bootjack watched him lope away. Pancho lifted his eyes and looked at Bootjack.

"I hope," Bootjack said, "that he remembers to bring her gun and her lawbadge."

And Pancho stared at him, not comprehending.

Books by Lee Floren
in the Linford Western Library:

BLACK GUNSMOKE
LOBO VALLEY
DEADLY DRAW
THE SADDLE WOLVES
SHOOT-OUT AT MILK RIVER
RIMROCK RENEGADE
THE HARD RIDERS
RUSTLER'S TRAIL

Other titles in the Linford Western Library:

Fargo the
road. The ambushers up ahead had now
blocked the road. Fargo's convoy was a
jumble, a perfect target for the insurgents'
weapons!

SUNDANCE:
DEATH IN THE LAVA
by John Benteen

The land echoed with the thundering hoofs of
Mc
do
car
cal
sw

Da
th
pe
hi
th
it.